WORLD CUP

STRIKERS

WORLD CUP

DAVID ROSS AND BOB CATTELL

MADCAP

First published in Great Britain in 2000
by Madcap Books,
André Deutsch Ltd,
76 Dean St,
London, W1V 5HA
www.vci.co.uk

Text copyright © 1999 Madcap Books/
David Ross and Bob Cattell

ISBN 0 233 00693 1

Typset by
Derek Doyle & Associates, Liverpool.
Printed by Mackays of Chatham plc

1
ENGLAND EXPECTS

It was the first of June and Thomas was worried.

The silly thing was that he ought to have been the happiest person in the world. He'd been picked for the England squad of 35 for the World Cup which started in just two weeks' time. He'd been playing well in the warm-up games and in training, and the England coach, Jacky Dooley, had told him privately that he was practically a cert for the final 22 which would be announced at the end of the week. The newspapers thought so too. Over the past few weeks every journalist who knew anything about football, and a lot more who didn't, had been selecting their England side for the tournament – and Thomas Headley's name appeared in every one of them. For Thomas, who had only come on as substitute in two England games – both of them friendlies – it was all rather hard to take in. He wanted to be an England player more than anything in the world, but he realised that fortune was fickle, especially on the football field, and although everyone was talking about him now, he could well be forgotten by the end of the week. He knew that all he could do was to take his chances when they came.

The Cup – the greatest show on Earth – was being held in the UK for the first time since 1966. That made it huge – the biggest sporting event ever, and the biggest media circus, too. The nation had gone completely, crazily football mad. Football was the only topic of conversation in pubs, restaurants, offices and homes throughout the land. Everything else in the world seemed to have come to a halt; all that mattered was the World Cup and the success of the England and Scotland teams. And that was partly what was worrying Thomas. It was why he'd come to have a chat with Joss Morecombe. Joss was the manager of Sherwood Strikers, Thomas's club, but, in the few short months that Thomas had been playing for Strikers, Joss had become much more than his manager: he looked upon him now as a true friend and mentor – a father almost.

'What you've got to remember, Thomas lad, is that English newspapers love to put you up on a flaming great pedestal just to practise their favourite sport of throwing custard pies at you. The higher you are the more they enjoy knocking you off or seeing you with egg on your face.

Never forget that.' Joss was leaning back in an old chair in the small, dark corner that he fondly called his room or his den but never his office. It was a scruffy little place tucked away in the middle of the Strikers' executive suite, crammed with armchairs, boxes, magazines, books and unidentifiable rubbish. Joss had chosen it in preference to his predecessor's impressive show office; it suited his approachable style.

The Strikers' manager looked like everyone's favourite uncle with his long, silver-grey hair and smiling eyes, and, indeed, he was a kind, thoughtful man with remarkably few enemies for someone in his position. But he played second fiddle to no one in the tough world of Premiership football. In Thomas's opinion Joss was the best, the most professional manager in the country. He knew more about football, and managing and motivating players, than anyone he'd ever met.

'What's troubling you then, son?' Joss always got straight to the point.

Thomas realised that he didn't know precisely what it was that was nagging away at him – or rather there were a number of things. He felt uneasy – as if something unpleasant was about to happen.

'Is it the England set-up?' continued Joss. 'Jack Dooley's a good coach, lad. As good as anyone in the country – except me perhaps.' The manager's big face creased into an enormous smile.

'Yeah, I know but . . .'

'But he's under a lot of pressure,' continued Joss. 'The whole ruddy country thinks his team's just got to show up and we'll walk away with the World Cup like we did back in the sixties. We know that's ridiculous. England haven't won so much as a silver spoon for years. At best we're top of the second league along with Nigeria and Spain. The favourites have got to be Brazil and Germany and France plus Holland, Italy and maybe Argentina. But you try telling that to the hacks. They've all been crowing about home advantage and England's destiny and all that twaddle. So now anything short of England winning 6–0 in the final will be considered the worst disaster since the Titanic went down. Poor old Jacky – I wouldn't want to be in his shoes.' He stopped and looked seriously at Thomas and then a glint came into his eyes and he spoke again in a quieter voice. 'That's not true. I'd give everything to manage England. I'd even give up Strikers for that one.'

'And I'd give anything to play just one game . . . but I wish . . .'

'Spit it out, son.'

'It's silly really but I've got this bad feeling about some of the players in the squad.'

'Drew Stilton bothering you again?' Drew played up front for Sherwood Strikers. He was only a few months older than Thomas, one of the young players whom Joss had introduced over the past season. He was a great talent but imma- ture and unpredictable and everyone knew there was no love lost between him and Thomas.

'No, it's not Drew for once,' said Thomas with a slightly self-mocking smile. 'But there are a couple of players in the squad who ... but it's probably nothing ...'

'You mean Micky Druitt and Zak Morgan?'

'How d'you know?'

'I know a lot more about what goes on at the England training camp than you think. Jack and me used to play together and he's a great one for running up big telephone bills. So I've heard all about the Druitt and Morgan boozing sessions. It baffles me. You get a chance to play for your country in the World Cup and you risk it all on a skinful or two down the boozer or the nightclub or wherever they misbehave. Zak Morgan's a nutcase. He may be a brilliant footballer but he's more likely to get sent off than our Dean Oldie – and that's saying something. Jacky Dooley'd do well to leave him out of the squad if you ask me. When's he picking the final 22?'

'After Sunday's game.' England had their final friendly before the tournament began against Denmark who hadn't qualified for the World Cup this time. The last so-called friendly had been a disaster. Switzerland had beaten them 2–1 at the Cockpit and, in a bad-tempered match, Byron

Balls, the first reserve goalie, had broken a thumb and the young midfield hope, Toussaint Bart-Hyde, had torn a hamstring. Both had waved goodbye to their chances of playing in the World Cup.

'There's something else, isn't there?' said Joss after a pause.

'Yeah. I've heard this rumour about the boss, about Jacky Dooley.'

'More press lies?'

'Maybe. But it was Katie Moncrieff who told me. She says there's a story going around that he was involved in some illegal contracts when he was managing Barbican.'

'Backhanders? You're kidding. No, Jack's not the type. He's not even interested in money – and when he's got some he gives it away before it burns a hole in his pocket. He's the last person to get his fingers caught in the "jack and jill". What's the lass been telling you?'

'She says the *Post* has got the story and they're planning to run it next week, just before the tournament starts.'

'That is worrying. The *Post* would do anything for a couple of extra readers. And, even though she's a journalist, I think I trust young Katie – not just because she's a friend of yours, mind.'

Katie Moncrieff was a football staff writer on the *Mirror*. She knew almost as much about football as Joss and she was a good reporter. Everyone at Strikers liked her except Drew Stilton who had fallen out with her when she was ghosting his book which never got published. Thomas included Katie amongst his closest friends. She was five years older than he was – he'd just turned 18 – but she didn't behave old.

'I'd better give Jack a bell,' said Joss Morecombe. 'From the sound of it he's going to need a good friend or two. The English press don't deserve a decent national football coach. And if I find out who's peddling this evil story I'll set the fans from the Park End on them and if they're lucky they'll finish up in a meat pie.'

Thomas felt a lot better for talking over his worries with Joss. On Thursday he'd be back at the England training camp again and – if he was picked for the squad – the pressure would start to build and build. By the time England played their first game on the 15th, it would be melt-down and Thomas feared the cracks would start to appear. Everything, it seemed, depended on the manager's selection for the final 22.

He drove home from the Trent Park ground in his red Saab convertible – it was barely 10 minutes' walk from the Strikers stadium but the club's security rules banned him from walking around town. As he pulled up outside his home in Nutberry Gardens his mobile rang.

'Hi, Thomas, Katie here. You've been talking to Joss Morecombe.'

'Hell, he doesn't waste any time.'

'It was a good idea. I'm going to run a story tomorrow to try and spike the *Post*. It's Joss's suggestion. He's talking to Jacky Dooley to get the facts. He knows it's risky – but it's better than the *Post* calling all the shots.'

'That'll be good for you too. Breaking the story first.'

'Maybe. I just hope there's no truth in it. There's talk of the *Post* having proof that Jacky's bent – a bank statement or something.'

'I'm sure he's not on the fiddle.'

'You never can tell. I can't say I'm looking forward to writing about it. I'd much rather stick to typing stuff about silly boys kicking a ball about. Do you think you'll make the team for the first one against Nigeria?'

'Hang on, I'm not even in the squad yet.'

'Let me tell you, Thomas, if you don't make the 22 there'll be riots throughout the land, except perhaps in Scotland where everyone's a bit saner and most people haven't even heard of you.'

'But I'm half Scottish.'

'Yeah, I know. I've never forgiven you for selling out. But seriously, if they pick Zak Morgan ahead of you, then I'll tear up all my Scotland World Cup tickets. If he plays he'll be the fattest and unfittest player ever to pull on a shirt in a World Cup tournament. Come to think of it, if he plays, Scotland will have a better chance of reaching the final. I'll ring you later. Bye.'

Thomas sat in his car for a few moments thinking, the base line of his favourite LL Cool J CD throbbing through the speakers. The World Cup wasn't going to be a problem for him – in spite of Zak Morgan and Micky Druitt and the *Post*, he was going to enjoy himself. He was feeling good, on top of his game and not an injury in sight. If the manager picked him, he'd play like he'd never played before.

2
THE STING

The headline 'England Manager Denies Graft Rumours' dominated the back page – and there was a piece on the front page of the *Mirror*, too. It caused an instant storm. Every newspaper, radio and TV station in the country demanded an interview with Jacky Dooley. The team, now together again for the final warm-up game, was besieged by journalists looking for an angle on the story. It was the worst possible preparation for the Denmark game and put an impossible strain on the already tense practice sessions. One reporter managed to get into the England camp disguised as a groundsman but Ashleigh Coltrane spotted him and he was unceremoniously ejected by a couple of bodyguards who looked as if they were closely related to Mike Tyson and Mr Blobby.

At lunchtime on Friday the FA called a press conference. It went quite well until Jacky lost his temper with Dermot Gudgeon, the journalist from the *Post* who, Katie said, was behind the whole story. Dermot provoked Jacky, calling him a crook in front of the cameras. The slanging match wasn't too serious but it didn't look good on the *Six O'Clock News*.

On Saturday evening Thomas and most of the other members of the squad went to the Association of Sportswriters' Awards Dinner. Security was tight and Jacky thought an evening of relaxation would calm the boys down. He himself kept well away, however, which was just as well because the buzz amongst the journalists was all about him and the alleged illegal transfer deals.

Katie Moncrieff was sitting at Thomas's table and she fended off question after question about her source for the Dooley story. Then the award ceremony began and with the very first announcement Thomas nearly fell off his chair.

'And the Young Footballer of the Year 1999 is . . . Thomas Headley of Sherwood Strikers.'

Thomas stared blankly. The eyes of the room were upon him and he couldn't move. It had never crossed his mind that he'd win an award.

'Come on, Thomas,' said Katie. 'They're waiting for you.'

Unsteadily Thomas walked towards the stage. It seemed to take ages. As he squinted into the lights, his silver trophy and his cheque in his hands, he realized to his horror that the audience expected him to make a speech. He mumbled a few words of thanks to Joss Morecombe, Len Dallal, the chief coach at Strikers, and his mother Elaine, who was also his manager. Jason Le Braz shouted, 'Great speech, mate!' and everyone laughed. On the way back to his seat he tripped over Drew Stilton's foot, which shot out 'accidentally' just at the moment he passed. Thomas stumbled and dropped his trophy. Furious with Drew and red faced he retrieved the award from under the table and noticed that it had a slight dent in it. Drew was grinning like an ape as he picked himself up.

The applause was still ringing out as he arrived back at his table and Katie gave him a big kiss. 'I voted for you,' she whispered. Then in a much louder voice she pronounced, 'Of course it was a two horse race between you and Graham Deek. There was no one else in the frame.' Drew heard every word and he scowled at her.

There were four players in their teens in the England squad and all were tipped to make the last 22. Both Thomas (who was just 18) and his friend Graham Deek (19), the Highfield Rovers striker, had been part of the England set-up for some months. Drew Stilton (18) and Jason Le Braz (19), Thomas's best mate at Sherwood, had only come into the reckoning for the national team after a run of form at the end of the season which included winning the FA Cup. Jason had been over the moon with his selection but Drew had just looked cool and said it was about time that his skills were recognised.

Drew was jealous of Thomas, simple as that – and it was pretty clear that the announcement of the Young Footballer of the Year had ruined his evening. He started to drink heavily and halfway through the awards ceremony he threw a glass of wine over a waiter. The assistant England coach, Dave Geddis, stepped in and calmed things down but it was lucky for Drew that Jacky Dooley wasn't there. Jacky had told the whole squad that it was a strictly no drinking evening and they were to be back at the hotel by 11 pm in good shape for tomorrow's game. Drew, it seemed, wasn't doing his chances of playing in the World Cup a lot of good.

The Sunday game against Denmark gave Jacky Dooley his last chance to test out the probable 11 for England's first World Cup draw against Nigeria – although the style of the top African opposition would be wildly different from the defensive Danes with their long-ball game.

Thomas was on the bench and the manager's starting line-up raised a few eyebrows amongst the press contingent. There was no Marty Mullett or Francie Ramsay – the two players hadn't been out of the England team for three seasons so it was hard to see what the manager was up to. No Thomas Headley or Drew Stilton either although the press had been promoting both of them hard since the end of the season. And Jacky was persevering with his 4–3–3 formation, too – even though it had failed so abysmally against Switzerland. Wasn't it a bit late, asked the tabloid reporters, to start experimenting with relatively untried players like Jamie Gopolan, who had two caps, and Freddy Dade, who had yet to play a full 90 minutes for England? What the *Post* actually said was: 'Two Steps Back for Wacky Jacky'.

This was the line-up against Denmark:

Reserves: Ally Spink, Jason Le Braz, Jimmy Stinger, Drew Stilton, Wes Dwyer, Francie Ramsay, Ray Clooney, Thomas Headley, Marty Mullett.

The regular skipper, Jimmy Stinger, was on the bench, nursing a slight muscle niggle he'd got in the Swiss game and so Bazza Taylor took over the captain's armband.

The first half was perhaps the most boring 45 minutes of football Thomas had ever watched. To be fair, the Danish emphasis on defence and man-to-man midfield marking didn't help. But the England team seemed to have no real ideas for breaking down the opposition. Playing Zak Morgan alongside Jamie Gopolan in midfield wasn't working. Zak looked slow and ponderous and he nearly gifted a breakaway goal to Denmark on the half hour. Two years ago Zak had been hailed as the English creative genius. He had one sizzling game against Scotland and then he got injured and the drink problems began to take over. The problem with Zak was that he wasn't fit. He could still make a pass of such precision and beauty that you'd almost weep for joy, but most of the time he wasted his talent and the pace of the international game was too much for him.

However, just on half time, after an anonymous first half, Zak whipped in a delightful cross from the left and Ashleigh Coltrane got a head to it and hit the crossbar. That was the nearest any player on the pitch had come to scoring.

Jacky Dooley made three changes at half time. Ally Spink replaced Sean Pincher in goal and

Francie Ramsay and Drew Stilton came on for
Jamie Gopolan and Graham Deek. Thomas
wondered whether he was part of the boss's plans
but he didn't say a word to the other subs. Then
after another 20 minutes of negative football he
got the nod.

'You're on for Miko Collins, Tommy,' said the
assistant coach Dave Geddis. 'The boss wants you
to stick out wide and get in the crosses. Marty's
coming on too to give us some extra height in the
box.'

Marty Mullett and Thomas switched with Miko
Collins and Freddy Dade and the biggest roar of
the afternoon went up from the crowd.

> 'Headley, oh Head-ley
> The greatest player in hist-or-y
> Ooh ah dead-ly
> Where's he been? It's a myst-er-y.'

Thomas grinned to himself – it was the first time
he'd heard the new chant. That's going to take
some living up to, he thought. With his first touch
of the ball, however, he forgot about the crowd
and he quickly picked up the pace of the game.
The Danish man-to-man marking was very physical and Thomas received a short-arm jab in the
chest and a kick on the thigh before he'd been on
for five minutes. Then he latched onto a through

ball from Rory Cameron and galloped past his marker to the dead-ball line. The whipped-in cross was met by Ashleigh Coltrane in full stride and he hammered the ball straight at the goalie when it would have been easier to score. The crowd groaned.

Two minutes later the Danes got a breakaway goal from a brilliant throughball and a lob which caught Ally Spink off his line. It was a killer punch and some of the England players' heads went down. Denmark massed in defence and there seemed to be no way through. The match had already gone into extra time and half the crowd was booing and the other half flooding out of the gates when, suddenly, with a beautifully weighted pass, Zak Morgan found Thomas in space on the left. He ran at his marker and this time cut inside, leaving him for dead. A second defender rushed at him and he side-stepped to the right again. For a brief second a space opened up between Thomas and the goal and he swung his right foot. The timing felt good and the ball curved viciously towards the top left angle of the Danish goal. The keeper's fingers may have brushed it against the upright but the pace of the shot took it in off the post. GOAL! Thomas stood dead still, his arms reaching out to the fans behind the goal. In sheer relief the other England players fell on him one by one.

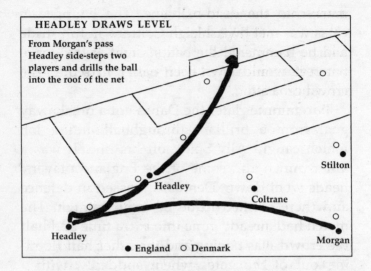

'Eng-er-land. Eng-er-land' chanted the crowd for the first time in the match and before the game could restart the ref blew for time.

'Left it a bit late, didn't you, Tommy?' grinned Ashleigh Coltrane. Thomas's Sherwood Strikers team-mate had missed two of the best chances in the game and that wasn't like Ashleigh. The last minute goal took the pressure off him a little – and he knew it. As they left the field the team got a mixed reception: lukewarm applause and a few boos. The players knew the press weren't likely to give them an easy ride after this performance and Jacky Dooley decided, rightly or wrongly, to refuse all interview requests apart from the compulsory TV appearance – and he kept that pretty brief too.

He was back in the dressing room before anyone had started to change.

'I just want you to know, lads, that, apart from the soft goal you gave away, I was pleased with that performance. We kept it tight and didn't lose our concentration.'

'Not enough urgency,' mumbled Francie Ramsay.

'Maybe not,' agreed the manager. 'But they're a difficult side to break down and we stuck to it. Now here's what you've been waiting for.' The manager held out a sheet of paper. 'I want you to know my decision before we go public with it. There are 22 names on this piece of paper because we're only allowed 22. Otherwise I'd pick the lot of you. But 13 of the squad we've had training together for nearly a month are going to be disappointed. I've had to make the choice and it wasn't easy. But this is it.' He read out the names.

Goal	Sean Pincher	Sherwood Strikers
	Ally Spink	Danebridge Forest
	Ferdy Melhuish	Kingstown Academy
Defence	Rory Cameron	White Hart United
	Dave Franchi	Sherwood Strikers
	Jason Le Braz	Sherwood Strikers
	Francie Ramsay	Danebridge Forest
	Bazza Taylor	Fenland Rangers (Vice Captain)
	Rutherford Stacey	Barbican
Midfield	Miko Collins	St James United

	Zak Morgan	St James United
	Jimmy Stinger	Highfield Rovers (Captain)
	Thomas Headley	Sherwood Strikers
	Ray Clooney	Barbican
	Jamie Gopolan	Border Town
Forwards	Graham Deek	Highfield Rovers
	Ashleigh Coltrane	Sherwood Strikers
	Freddy Dade	Highfield Rovers
	Drew Stilton	Sherwood Strikers
	Marty Mullett	Barbican
	Henderson Springer	West Thames Wanderers
	Wes Dwyer	St James

Jason Le Braz looked at Thomas, his eyes gleaming. 'What a turn up,' he said. 'Three months ago I couldn't even get in to the Strikers first team – and now I'm in the England World Cup squad.' He grabbed Thomas by the arms and shook him.

'Wait till I tell Elaine and Richie,' said Thomas and then he blushed, thinking perhaps he shouldn't admit that his first thoughts were for his mother and little brother.

'That's six Strikers players in the squad,' said Jason. 'Twice as many as St James and Barbican.'

Ashleigh Coltrane, Dave Franchi and Sean Pincher all came over to congratulate Thomas and Jason. Sean and Ashleigh were regulars in the England side and Dave had played four full internationals. But the sixth Strikers player sat stubbornly in his corner of the dressing room. Drew Stilton would swim through shark-infested seas before he'd congratulate Thomas Headley.

Thomas took another look at the list. No Micky Druitt. But Zak had made the side – in spite of his fitness problems. The shortage of creative midfielders in the country had probably swayed the boss's decision.

The afternoon ended in a big singsong in the shower. The game they had just finished was forgotten and the players were already thinking ahead to the real thing – England v Nigeria at Wembley – the first of the big ones. The qualifying leagues for the World Cup had given England a tough draw but, at least, if they got past France and the other results went to form, they were unlikely to meet either of the favourites, Brazil or Germany, before the semi-finals.

This was the draw for the World Cup:

Group A	Group B
England	Argentina
Nigeria	Slovakia
United States	Norway
France	Australia

Group C	Group D
Germany	Brazil
Mexico	Scotland
South Africa	Cameroon
Spain	Japan

Group E	Group F
Italy	Holland
China	Chile
Morocco	Turkey
Portugal	Russia

Only group winners are guaranteed a place in the quarter-finals. They will be joined by the two second placed teams with the highest number of points (or most goals scored in the case of a dead heat).

3
GOLDEN OPPORTUNITY

'My brother Thomas is in the World Cup squad! My brother Thomas is in the World Cup squad!' The big smile on Richie Headley's face said it all, as he burst out of the front door to greet Thomas who had just arrived home in his Saab. He had a few hours to sort out his business affairs with Elaine before he reported back to the England camp.

'My brother Thomas is in the World Cup squad. He's playing for England,' chanted Richie.

'Hold on, little brother,' said Thomas. 'I'm only in the 22. I'm not picked for the team yet.'

'You will be,' said Richie with all the confidence of a 12 year old. Elaine, their mother, arrived to greet Thomas, too. With a huge smile she gave both of her sons a hug. For some time, at least, she could see there would be no football rivalry in the Headley household. Richie, a big Highfield

Rovers supporter, was already signed up for the Highfield youth team and he and Thomas rarely missed a chance to play Sherwood Strikers off against Rovers. Now there was a truce – the brothers were united in their desire to see England win the Jules Rimet trophy for the first time since 1966.

Thomas didn't have much time, however, to celebrate his elevation to the England squad and he and Elaine got down to work. Elaine had been his agent virtually since he'd arrived at Sherwood Strikers. It was a bit unusual to have your mother as your manager and some of the Strikers players teased him about it. But Elaine and Thomas trusted each other completely and not one of the other agents could boast of being more professional at the job. Together they sorted through the interviews, the charity requests and the commercial deals until they came to the one that really interested Thomas.

'Did you look at the Club Striker agreement?' he asked.

'Well . . . yes.'

'And did you like it?'

'I'm not sure.'

Club Striker was a new chain of up-market soccer restaurants which was about to be launched in three prime city-centre sites before going nationwide. Big screen live matches, football concessions, meeting and eating with the stars, computer games, table football – Thomas thought it had everything.

'Club Striker? Is it anything to do with Strikers? Does the club have a stake in it?' asked Elaine.

'Don't think so,' said Thomas. 'Jason and Little Mac reckon it's a winner. And there are several other Strikers players thinking of investing in it too.'

'Who?'

'Well er . . . Drew Stilton.'

'Drew Stilton? Since when have you been keen to go into business with Drew Stilton?'

'It's not like going into business. We'd be investors and sponsors. There'll be other players too from all the Premiership clubs. Fifty thousand pounds sounds a good deal to me.'

'It's a lot of money – and a big risk.'

'Risk? It can't go wrong. And if it goes public, the sky's the limit – the shareholders could make millions.'

'I'd like to know more about it,' said Elaine. 'Like who's behind it. What does Joss Morecombe think about it?'

'Joss Morecombe? I haven't asked him.' There was a hint of impatience creeping into Thomas's voice. 'What's it to do with him?'

'Well he might know who's managing it, for a start. We need more information, Thomas.'

'I think it's Little Mac's manager's idea. Arun Canin – have you heard of him?'

'Yes. He's just taken over as Drew Stilton's agent, too. I don't think he's been in football for very long – he's a bit of a mystery figure. I'll ask Joss about him and then we can talk about it again,' said Elaine. 'Right now I'm too busy for new business ventures. Ever since you got into the England squad, the phone and the fax have been red-hot. By the way, Pete Frame rang from the Strikers press office. As a favour to him I said you'd do a five-minute chat on Sherwood Metro tomorrow morning.'

'A favour to him? A favour to slimy Barney Haggard, more likely,' said Thomas. Barney Haggard was the star presenter of the local radio chat show and not a popular person at Strikers. But Thomas knew he had to do all he could to promote the club locally.

His mobile rang.

'Hi, is that Deadly Headley the English Ronaldo?' said the voice at the other end. 'Say, you'd better get up early in the morning and start training cos the Americans are coming to kick butt.'

'Rory!' Thomas's voice rose to a shout.

'Guess who's number one goalkeeper for the old US of A?' said Rory.

Rory Betts was Strikers' reserve keeper and, along with Jason, Thomas's best buddy in the team. He was calling from the American training camp in the north east. The US team were in the same league as England and the two teams were scheduled to play on Saturday after England's game with Nigeria.

'I can't believe it,' said Thomas. 'Haven't they got any goalies in the States?'

'If you play for England against us, I'll make you wish you'd never said that,' said Rory with a laugh. 'And do you know where we're playing?'

'At Trent Park.'

'Right. It'll be a home tie for both of us, only you and I will be facing in opposite directions. See you then. Good luck.'

Thomas smiled to himself. He knew Rory had been worried about being left out of the American squad because of his lack of world-class experience and he was delighted for his friend – somehow it made the World Cup feel like a family affair. Brad Trainor, the Strikers' full back, was also in the US team and Jamie MacLachlan was captain of the Scottish team; Cozzie Lagattello and Sergio Gambolini were playing for Italy and Francisco Panto-Gomes was representing Portugal. Twelve Strikers players in the World Cup – no other team in the world came close to that.

The days passed slowly in the countdown to the tournament. The opening game was between Brazil, the holders, and Scotland. Poor old Scotland, it seemed that they were forever fated to play Brazil in the opening game of the World Cup. Thomas had bet Katie Moncrieff of the *Mirror* £10 that Scotland would let in at least three goals.

But there were still five days to wait until then and meanwhile the training and the interviews and sponsorship commitments continued to fill the players' time. The publishers of the official tie-in England book wanted a new action picture of Thomas. The makers of the official World Cup cola wanted him to come to their press conference along with England skipper Jimmy Stinger. There was World Cup soap, World Cup chocolate, World Cup soup and World Cup underpants.

The England training camp at Chiving Beacon was becoming more and more claustrophobic and it was with relief that Thomas and Jason escaped one evening to a little club a few miles away. They'd arranged to meet Katie Moncrieff there and the three sat in a dark corner, away from the crowds, and let the music pound around them. Katie listened sympathetically to their stories of endless interviews, photo calls, pep talks, video sessions, down-the-line chats, product endorsements and personal appearances.

'One of these days we're going to look up at the sun,' said Jason, 'and find "Official World Cup Daylight Supplier" stamped right across it.'

'The whole thing's just a great circus for the fat

cats,' said Katie. 'They don't care about football; their only interest is in making money out of it. But still you've got to admit it's really exciting, isn't it?'

'Too right,' said Thomas. 'But I wish it would start. This endless waiting's driving me nuts.'

'Look out, here comes trouble,' said Jason suddenly.

Two figures approached through the haze of light. One was short and dumpy, the other tall and lanky. Thomas recognised them immediately. The short and dumpy one suddenly gave out an evil, ear-drum splitting squeal.

'Look,' cried Milly Valentini. 'It's Tommo and Jace.' She clutched the hand of her companion and they both looked as if they were going to scream again. Thomas and Jason put their hands over their ears.

'It's him all right,' said Lercher with a giggle. Milly Valentini and Lucia Robson, known to the Strikers players as 'Mills and Goon' but to each other as 'Milly' and 'Lercher', were two of Sherwood's most faithful fans. They never missed a game or a training session or a chance to chat to the boys. Or, more accurately, Milly chatted and Lercher stood next to her sniffing.

'Time to be going,' murmured Thomas to Katie. He didn't really mind the two girls but he wasn't in the mood to talk to them tonight. What were they doing here anyway? Probably official World

Cup groupies to the England team, thought Thomas with a smile to himself.

'Mind if we sit here?' asked Milly, placing herself next to Jason. Lercher slid in beside her, darting furtive glances at the two boys. Milly meanwhile reached into her handbag, brought out a mobile and rapidly dialled a number.

'Dottie? Is that you, Dottie? Hey, guess who we're with? You'll never – THOMAS HEADLEY AND JACE LE BRAZ! No, honest.' She suddenly held out the mobile to Thomas. 'Go on, will ya? Do us a favour. Just say hello to my mate Dottie. She's on late shift at Sainsbury's.'

'Hello, Dottie,' said Thomas, holding the mobile as he got to his feet. 'We're just off home to bed. Good night.'

He, Jason and Katie eased themselves through the dancing masses and found their way to the cars.

'Have you heard about Joss Morecombe?' asked Katie as Thomas was saying good night.

'What about him?'

'He's joining the England camp as Dooley's Number Two.'

'You sure?'

'Yeah, I think Jacky Dooley's decided he needs some help, particularly with all this financial scandal stuff flying about. Good choice, if you ask me.' She showed Thomas and Jason the sports pages of her advance copy of the next day's

Mirror which lay on the front seat of her car. The headline read: 'BIG JOSS STEPS UP FOR ENGLAND ROLE'. The story, with Katie's by-line, explained that the Strikers' manager was offering his services free of charge to the embattled England coach. 'I'll do whatever Jack asks,' Morecombe was quoted as saying. 'Even if it's handing round the tea and biscuits. There is nothing more important to English football than this tournament. I'm a total believer in Jack Dooley's ability and I'll do whatever I can to help him and the side.' Katie summed it up. 'It takes a big man to make a stand like this,' she wrote. 'At a stroke he will have put fresh heart into the team. He already manages six of the squad and his experience will lift all the players. No one else in English football would have made this gesture – and there was nobody else whom Jacky Dooley would have accepted. That is the measure of these two men.'

'Good news,' said Jason quietly as the two England colleagues drove out of the car park.

'Great news,' agreed Thomas.

4
GOAL FEAST

The World Cup opening ceremony came and went. Apart from marching around Wembley in their tracksuits which got a bit boring, most of the England team enjoyed it. There was a big thrill in representing your country on the world stage. The show featured a brilliant performance by 100 parascenders wearing the colours of the competing countries, a strange dance routine featuring Chinese dragons and English bulldogs, which got a bit out of hand, and a good concert which starred Suzi Verv, Rara Avis and the three tenors. The tenors, a fat one, a tall one and a short one, always seemed to get in on the act at the World Cup though they were probably all about a hundred now. Thomas enjoyed the singing, however – especially the Toreador song from Carmen which was one of Elaine's favourites.

Back at the Chiving Beacon camp to watch the Brazil v Scotland game the England players were beginning to feel part of a large family. At first the intensity and detail of the preparations had come as a shock, to the younger players particularly. In the England youth team they'd suffered under the bumbling leadership of 'Donkey' Donkins and maybe some, Thomas included, had thought the national team would not be very different. They'd soon learnt otherwise.

'After this, we could take on the SAS,' joked Graham Deek to Thomas. They had finished a long training workout in the gym, a 45-second cold splash and 90-second hot shower before turning out on the pitch to work on set pieces and close ball skills.

As well as the team programmes, each player had his own detailed diagnostic chart and work-sheet highlighting special needs, abilities or failings. Thomas had a programme for stretching and strengthening his hamstrings which were always liable to give him trouble. Never had he been so worked over, pummelled and kneaded by the physios. Jacky Dooley's little army of specialists asked no questions and worked like beavers. And Jacky and Joss Morecombe were never far away from the action. Joss was having the time of his life. Under the eyes of the two managers England were building into the best-prepared side in the competition, mentally and physically. Outside the England camp World Cup madness continued. But inside all was workman-like, professional and utterly committed. Thomas Headley felt that way, anyway. And he knew he wasn't alone.

But the calm wasn't destined to last. As the team came in for lunch after their final training session they were met by a bombshell. Dave Geddis handed Jacky Dooley the *Evening News* and within minutes they had all read the story.

'ENGLAND SCUM!' screamed the headline on the front page. And below it were the bleary features of Zak Morgan and Wes Dwyer. Another picture showed a man with a black eye and a battered saxophone. The two players had trashed a club in North London after a dispute about which of them would play a saxophone solo with the band. The regular saxophonist had told them to clear off and, according to him, Zak had smashed his instrument and punched him in the face and Wes had put his foot through the bass drum.

'It was only bit of fun,' Dwyer protested as Jacky and Joss immediately tackled him and Zak Morgan about the article.

'You mean it's true?' screamed Joss. 'What the hell were you doing at a night-club?'

Thomas and Jason looked at each other. Clubbing was strictly out of bounds to all the squad, although nearly everyone crept off for a bit of relaxation from time to time. That didn't mean getting involved in punch-ups, though.

Zak Morgan looked at Joss defiantly. 'We go where we like. We're not children.'

'I wouldn't bet on it,' whispered Joss.

'I'll see you both in my office now,' said Jacky Dooley. And that was the last that the rest of the squad saw of Zak and Wes for the duration of the World Cup. They were packed off home and Jacky immediately called a press conference to explain the action he'd taken. It meant that the England squad was now down to 20 players. More significantly, they'd lost a midfielder and a striker – the two areas where the squad was weakest.

Zak Morgan, fit and on form, could always be a match winner. Jacky Dooley knew that, without him, some of the magic had drained away from the team; the magic that the fat fool could create when he wanted.

'No good worrying about what can't be,' Joss told Jacky. 'I see him as a luxury you couldn't afford.'

'I'm not sure we've got a player to take his place, though,' said Jacky gloomily. 'Zak had class. You can't train that into anyone. It leaves us exposed creatively, you know.'

'Maybe. So we'll have to look for combinations of players. Take Deek and Headley. Sometimes, when I watch them together, I think they're almost telepathic. Deek in front, and Headley nicking in just behind – they each seem to know exactly what the other is going to do. They make their own space. I've seen it happen.'

'You might be right,' said Jacky Dooley. 'But what a risk. What a gamble on youth and inexperience.'

'You'll see. Those lads won't let you down.'

Along with hundreds of millions of others throughout the world, the England squad watched the Brazil v Scotland game on television. The crowd at the new Forth Stadium was magnificent, the atmosphere electric – so it was almost to be expected that the game itself was a huge disappointment as a spectacle. It ended in an uninspiring 0–0 draw. But the Scots were over the moon at the result. Hoards of kilted supporters flooded on to the pitch at the end and the Strikers players were delighted to watch Jamie MacLachlan, the Sherwood and Scotland captain, running off the pitch the proudest man alive.

'That was a great game for Big Mac,' said Sean Pincher afterwards. 'Man of the Match without a doubt.'

'He completely controlled it,' said Dave Franchi. 'If only Big Mac were English.'

'Then you'd never get a game, Dave,' said Jimmy Stinger.

'No worry, mate. If England wins, I'm happy – playing or not playing,' said Dave.

The game was hardly over when Katie called Thomas to demand her £10. He thought she sounded a little drunk.

Wembley held no terrors for Thomas. It was not so long since he had run round the touchline of the illustrious ground with the FA Cup in his hands. The unforgettable final against Highfield Rovers had made Wembley a lucky ground for him and he was going to keep it that way.

That didn't mean that he didn't feel nervous. He had the biggest knot in his stomach he could remember as he ran out of the tunnel with Ashleigh Coltrane immediately in front of him and Graham Deek behind. He still couldn't quite believe that the boss had given him the nod for the Nigeria game. Thomas Headley playing for England at Wembley in the World Cup! It was just too much to take in.

Jacky Dooley had announced the team to the squad on the previous evening. The press didn't hear about it until just before the game. That was Jacky's style – to make sure the players were in the know before everyone else.

So when the England line-up ran onto the pitch, Thomas Headley's inclusion was greeted with a roar of approval from the England supporters. This was the team:

Reserves: Ally Spink (goal), Francie Ramsay, Jamie Gopolan, Drew Stilton, Freddy Dade.

The 4–3–2–1 system showed the distinctive mark of Joss Morecombe. It was one of his favourite formations at Strikers, particularly for away games. And although this was no away game, it was vital that England didn't concede an early goal. Soak up the pressure and threaten on the break was the message.

Nigeria were a team with daunting skill and talent, the champions of Africa, packed with footballing legends who had made their names playing for the top European sides – players like the towering Choma Ekinki and the brilliant little winger, Zachy Olawande. Their captain, Wole Ahime, had promised he would take the Cup to

Africa for the first time and Nigeria certainly had the talent to do just that.

As he stood waiting for the kick-off – the national anthems and the presentations over at last – Thomas looked at the Nigerian players one by one. They appeared what they were: supremely fit and confident. I wonder how we look to them, he thought. Then all became a whirl of activity as the Danish referee blew his whistle to start the match.

The Wembley crowd let out the greatest roar Thomas had ever heard as the pitch instantly exploded into a whirlwind of action. The Nigerian strategy was exactly as expected – to use their strength and pace to attack the English, especially down the wings. The England back four defended against cross after cross and it only seemed a matter of time before one of the tall Nigerians stuck one of them in the back of the net. Ekinki hit the cross bar and then Sean Pincher tipped over a vicious drive by the Nigerian captain.

We're not taking control of this game, Thomas thought to himself as he struggled to keep up with the pace. They're pulling us all over the place.

Then, completely against the run of play, Jimmy Stinger rose to block yet another cross and the ball fell to Marty Mullett, who had pulled back and was unmarked. Marty darted forward and, as three heavies closed in on him, he slipped through a delicate pass for Graham Deek to run on to. Thomas was on a diagonal run from the left and Deekie spotted him and back-heeled the ball. The whole Nigerian defence went the wrong way for a second and Thomas raced onto the ball and fired in a stinging drive from 20 yards. The keeper got a hand to it but the force of the shot carried it past him into the back of the net. There was a roar which almost knocked Thomas over. It shook his whole body and then his team-mates were there, congratulating him, and all other sounds were drowned out by the joyous chant of the crowd from behind the goal.

'Headley, oh Headley
Everybody knows he's deadly
Sing, sing, whatever you do
Sing for Tommy to give us two!'

The Nigerians were stung by the opportunist goal and the bombardment of the England box redoubled. Somehow the back four, with Sean behind them, kept them out. Then with the first half drawing to a close the tricky Zachy Olawande went on a run which took him past three players. He was eventually brought down by Bazza Taylor, just inside the area. The England players hardly protested at the penalty decision and the skipper, Wole Ahime, slotted the ball home low to Sean's left. A minute later the little winger served up another delightfully weighted cross and this time Choma Ekinki for once rose above Big Dave Franchi and headed the ball into the top corner of the net. Sean had no chance.

So England went in at half time a disappointing 1–2 down – a fair reflection of the play, perhaps, but they had lost the lead in two vital minutes when perhaps their minds were drifting towards the half-time break.

Jacky Dooley did his best to build them up again during the interval and he was full of praise for the back four and the midfield. 'I want to see a bit more readiness to support Ashleigh up front, in the next 45,' he said. 'We've got them worried about our speed on the left flank – let's link up and make the most of it.'

As they were filing out of the dressing room Joss Morecombe had a quiet word with Thomas. 'Tell Deekie to keep the movement down the left as wide as possible. Stretch them a bit. They're not as confident in defence as they are going forward. It's up to you and Deek to take the strain off the back four. Good luck, lad.'

Thomas grinned. They were a goal down but he was enjoying himself in spite of the gruelling physical nature of the game. But five minutes after half time Nigeria went 3–1 up thanks to another fierce volley from Ekinki. England retaliated with a goal from a set piece – struck beautifully over the wall from the edge of the area by Ashleigh Coltrane. 3–2 and game on once more.

In the 75th minute, Jacky Dooley brought on Freddy Dade for Marty Mullett who was limping slightly and suddenly England began to attack down the right wing as well as the left. A lovely cross from Freddy resulted in a goal mouth scramble and Deekie stuck out a foot and slid the ball over the line.

Now, with the scores level, the tactics and the control began to disappear. It became end to end stuff, like a local derby. The crowd fuelled the excitement with a barrage of noise as they roared England on to victory. Thomas was still linking well with Graham Deek down the left and a one-two along the touchline gave him a chance to break for the dead-ball line. His cross found the head of Jimmy Stinger who was racing in, and the ball fair rocketed into the back of the net.

4–3, and they were into extra time. The Nigerians swept forward again. The power and fitness of their front runners was awesome and the England backs were wilting under the pressure. After a break down the left, in came the cross. Sean Pincher parried the header but only to the feet of Zachy Olawande who hoofed the ball joyously into the roof of the net. The England players' heads dropped and the whistle blew for time.

The terrible disappointment that they had

failed to hang on to the three points hung heavy in the changing room afterwards. Jacky said all the right things but one or two of the players were blaming themselves. Dave Franchi and Rory Cameron were particularly quiet and gloomy. But Thomas had the memory of his first goal for England – and what a great goal it had been. And, after all, the draw wasn't a total disaster. They had secured a point and England were expected to beat the US. So, as predicted, everything would hang on the French game. It could have been a lot worse.

5
A FAST BUCK

Back at the Chiving Beacon camp, the English players had a chance to relax around the pool and reflect on some of the other results in the tournament. Apart from the Brazil v Scotland draw the big surprises so far were Slovakia's 2–1 win against Argentina and South Africa's victory over Spain at the City Ground.

These were the results after the first round of matches:

Group A
England 4 Nigeria 4
United States 0 France 1

Group B
Argentina 1 Slovakia 2
Norway 3 Australia 2

Group C
Germany 2 Mexico 1
South Africa 2 Spain 1

Group D
Brazil 0 Scotland 0
Cameroon 4 Japan 2

Group E
Italy 1 China 0
Morocco 1 Portugal 3

Group F
Holland 2 Chile 0
Turkey 2 Russia 2

France had got the expected three points against the Americans but it hadn't been easy and it had taken a disputed penalty to separate the two sides. Jason and Thomas rang up Rory after the game.

'Pity you had to go and let in an easy penalty,' said Jason, taunting his Strikers team-mate. 'I suppose the Frogs offered you a year's supply of champagne to dive over it.' The match reports said Rory had played a blinder and that the score might easily have been 6–0 without his dazzling contribution.

'Yeah, is your mother French or something?' asked Thomas grabbing the phone.

'Listen, Headley, there's no way England are going through to the next round now. We've got a big surprise for you on Saturday – mark my words.'

'If America beats us I'll hang up my boots and take up train spotting,' said Thomas.

'And I'll wave to you out of the wagon window as we steam towards Wembley for the Final.'

'So that's what they call the American dream. Dream on, buddy.'

'I enjoyed that goal of yours,' said Rory, in a quieter, more serious voice.

'Thanks,' said Thomas. 'It felt good. I hope there are more where that came from.'

Jason took the phone again and he and Rory began to talk about meeting up after the Saturday game at Trent Park. Then the conversation turned to the Club Strikers venture. Both Jason and Rory had been invited to invest £50,000 in the project and Rory was really keen.

'I can't see how it can go wrong for us. It's a brilliant idea and with football becoming more and more popular and all the kids wanting to eat out in fashionable restaurants, what more could you ask for?'

'I've already signed up,' said Jason. 'It isn't easy to scrape together £50K but I reckon it'll be worth at least double in six months. That's what Drew Stilton thinks – and, whatever you think of Drew, if someone as mean and selfish as him is keen to part with his money, it's got to be a good deal. Drew may be the most arrogant person in the world, but he's no sucker.'

Thomas listened to them talking. He usually allowed himself to be guided by Elaine in these things but she was taking so long to make up her mind. She had a lot on at the moment with Thomas away at the England camp and all the contracts for the new season under review. But then again, he didn't want to be the only one amongst his friends who missed out on this brilliant deal. Arun Canin had made it clear that he couldn't wait for ever. There were other people ready and waiting to take part if Thomas was hesitating.

Jason put the phone down. 'Rory's signing up today. What about you?'

'Well, yeah. Why not?' I can sign my own cheques without Elaine's permission, he thought.

He faxed Arun Canin for a copy of the agreement that afternoon and faxed back the signed form. He was really looking forward to being part owner of the smartest restaurant chain in the country. He'd take Katie along to the opening. All his mates would be there – it would be a great night.

Meanwhile, preparations in the England camp for Saturday's game were gathering pace. Marty Mullett's calf injury was worse than it had appeared – he'd be out for at least one game – and Rory Cameron had gone down with a stomach bug, so Jacky Dooley was forced to shuffle his already depleted pack.

'I'm worried about the defence with Rory out. He gives us a lot of mobility,' he confessed to Joss.

'I don't want to sound biased towards the Strikers players, but what about giving young Jason a run out?' said Joss.

'He's a bit right-footed and I need someone on the left. I think I prefer Francie Ramsay; he's got that extra touch of experience.'

'You're the boss.'

'And I'm bringing Freddy Dade into midfield and playing 4–4–2 against the Yanks. I thought we were weak in the middle on Wednesday and Freddy's got the class to play wide on the left. He's a two-footed player.'

'Yes, but that pushes Thomas inside and makes it more difficult for him to link up with young Graham.'

'It's a risk, I know. What would you do?'

'Probably the same as you,' said Joss with a diplomatic smile. 'You can always bring on Gopolan or Clooney as subs and push Headley wide again. He's got the pace; we've seen that.'

'Don't worry, I'm a convert. The lad could well be one of the stars of the tournament. But he needs nursing – he's still young and too big a workload at that age can be a killer. I've seen it happen.'

Jacky's team sheet for the game against the States looked like this:

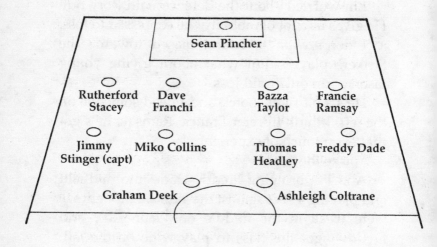

The team was in buoyant mood travelling on the coach to Sherwood. The two lost points against Nigeria had been pushed to the back of their minds. The press had been kind to them too. Katie in the *Mirror* called it the match of the tournament so far, and only the *Post* had put the boot in – describing Jacky Dooley's team selection and tactics as 'the wacky choices of a man with other things on his mind'. If the veiled reference to the so-called financial scandal wasn't enough, the article then went on to say that Jacky had been interviewed twice by the police – which was a complete lie – and that he had opened a Swiss bank account, which was an even bigger whopper.

The coach pulled into the Trent Park ground and parked alongside the US team coach. For Joss and the six Strikers players – Drew and Jason were on the bench – it was like a homecoming. Len Dallal, the Strikers trainer, and old smoothie Pete Frame, the press officer, were there to greet them, as were Elaine and Richie Headley. Katie Moncrieff was there too, talking to Pete; she waved at Thomas and gave him a thumbs up sign.

'Brilliant goal!' screamed Richie before Thomas was off the coach. Thomas gave his little brother the present he'd been keeping for him – the Nigerian shirt which he'd swapped with Zachy Olawande at the end of the game. It was worth it to see the look of sheer delight which spread over the 12 year old's face. 'You mean it's mine? To keep? Really?'

'I'll give you one from every game I play in, if you like,' said Thomas. 'But that's probably the only one that'll fit you. I don't think Zachy's much bigger than you.'

'He's brilliant,' said Richie. 'Can you get Dale Yelverton's shirt today and Cézanne Jacques's in the French game, please?'

'I'll try.'

Thomas had very little time to talk to Elaine and Richie before the team disappeared into the familiar home dressing room. Elaine wished him good luck and, as he was walking away, she said, 'Oh Thomas, while I remember – about that Club Striker business. I've been checking up on Arun Canin – and I'm not at all happy. I'll tell you why later.'

Thomas changed into his England away strip somewhat thoughtfully. What had Elaine meant? Was there something wrong with the venture? Surely not, if Little Mac, Jason, Rory and Drew were all supporting it? He tried to clear his mind and concentrate on the game ahead.

The US team had a useful midfield trio of Dale Yelverton, who played for Border Town, Dino Scarlatti and Walt Cumberland – both of whom were currently playing in Germany. And, of course, Brad Trainor, the Strikers star, was the pillar of their defence.

No one expected America to be a pushover; there were no easy teams in the World Cup any more. The 4–4–2 plan was designed to give scope for the outside halves – Freddy Dade on the left and Jimmy Stinger on the right – to break down the wings and link up with Ashleigh and Deekie up front. Thomas's role was a little deeper than in the Nigeria match. It wasn't his favourite position.

The American game plan was clear after only a few minutes had been played. They were getting everyone behind the ball except for Brandon Weinberg, who had the lone striker role. Their first priority was not to concede a goal.

Thomas was man-marked by Walt Cumberland who gave him a tough time and there was very little room for the England players to build their attacks. The US midfield trio and the back five gave no one more than a split second on the ball and the result was a scrappy and, at times, bad tempered first half. Ashleigh Coltrane was booked for a 'dive' in the penalty area. It was unlike Ashleigh to dive and Thomas suspected that Brad Trainor had given him a little shove but Ashleigh undoubtedly made a meal of it and his name went in the book. Then Rutherford Stacey, Jimmy Stinger and Dave Franchi got yellow cards in quick succession along with two of the Americans. None of the offences were serious – a push, a tackle marginally from behind and so on

– but this referee was taking no prisoners.
Thomas knew he would have to be very careful to
keep a clean record.

The game was one-way traffic towards the US
goal and they defended dourly. Ashleigh got a
shot on goal but Rory saved acrobatically, tipping
the ball over the bar. Then he pulled off an amazing reaction save to a Graham Deek close header
and, seconds later, dived at Jimmy Stinger's feet
to deny the England skipper. He was really enjoying himself and he gave Thomas a broad grin
after the third save.

Just before half time Freddy Dade got round
Dale Yelverton on the left wing for the first time in
the game and Deekie rose in the area to meet his
cross. He headed back and down firmly to
Ashleigh who was running in just yards away
with his marker on his shoulder. The ball bobbled
up and caught Ashleigh on his hand; it dropped in
front of him and he hit it on the half volley. The
shot was true and straight and, from that distance,
Rory had no chance. The roar of the England
crowd greeting the long-awaited goal was cut
short by the ref's whistle. He indicated hand ball,
walked over to Ashleigh, produced a yellow card,
then a red one and pointed to the exit.

Ashleigh couldn't believe what he was seeing.
He was being sent off in the World Cup. 'There's
no way that was a deliberate hand ball, ref,' he
screamed. 'It just hit my hand.'

The ref stood his ground and waved the red card again angrily. As the crowd booed, Jimmy Stinger came over and put an arm round Ashleigh's shoulder. The two of them walked towards the touch line with Ashleigh still shaking his head and saying, 'It hit my hand. It hit my hand.' The whistle went for half time and the rest of the team trooped off grimly behind him. The boos and jeers of the fans were mainly for the referee but the England performance had been a big disappointment to them, too.

6
SOME PEOPLE NEVER LEARN

The second half couldn't have begun in worse fashion for the ten men of England. Jacky Dooley was forced to make a couple of substitutions and the new formation left Deekie playing a lone role up front with Jamie Gopolan slotting into the gap in front of the midfield. Thomas dropped back further still and Rory Cameron, in spite of his

Sean Pincher

Rory Cameron   Dave Franchi   Bazza Taylor   Francie Ramsay

Jimmy Stinger (capt)   Miko Collins   Thomas Headley

Jamie Gopolan

Graham Deek

stomach upset, came on at the back for Rutherford who was visibly tiring towards the end of the first half and was now on two yellow cards for the tournament, which meant he'd miss the next game.

Before Rory could get the pace of the game he was beaten down the wing and the centre was met by Brandon Weinberg coming in at a gallop. Sean in goal was lined up well behind the header but the ball took a wicked deflection off Bazza Taylor's shoulder and defeated the keeper. There was a deadly silence and then the little pocket of American fans at the far end began to cheer and wave their stars and stripes banners. Astonishingly England had gone 0–1 down to one of the outsiders in the competition.

The ten men of England battled on but the US players got behind the ball and, although Deekie had two good shots on goal, Rory Betts between the posts pulled off magnificent saves again. Thomas found himself shadowed everywhere by Walt Cumberland and when they both went for a 50-50 ball, Thomas was booked by the ref for an unfair tackle. The decision should have gone the other way because he'd got to the ball first and Walt had caught him on the ankle. With anger rising up inside him, Thomas turned away from the ref – knowing that if he challenged the decision he'd probably be sent off.

With just minutes to play Jacky brought on

Drew Stilton for Miko Collins. Thomas went into the centre and Jamie Gopolan dropped back into midfield. With his first touch off the ball Drew found Thomas running down the left. He went past the right full back and struck a surprise shot at the American goal from all of 30 yards. The ball took a vicious dip at the last moment and Rory Betts was forced to dive to his left. He made the save but the best he could do was to parry the ball away and, before he could grab it to his chest, Drew was on to it. He lobbed it over the sprawling keeper and with a little leap followed it into the back of the net. Drew was delirious, Rory devastated. Thomas almost felt sorry for his friend, particularly when he heard Drew immediately bragging, 'See what I mean? Two touches of the ball and I score. What more can you ask?'

The ref blew the final whistle and Rory sank to his knees, head in hands.

'Never mind, mate,' said Thomas, giving him a pat on the back. 'If it hadn't been for you we'd have scored a dozen.'

'I guess you deserved the draw,' said Rory generously. 'But what a win that would have been. One minute less and we'd have whooped you.'

'Good shot though, wasn't it?' said Thomas with a grin. Rory forced a smile, too and they walked off arm in arm.

*

Back at their base at Chiving Beacon the England team tried to rebuild its confidence after the disappointments of the two early games. It was hard to get away from a feeling that things were falling apart. Some of the players were moody and disconsolate. Not Drew Stilton, though – he was full of himself and prepared to tell anyone who would listen just how Jacky Dooley should go about picking the side. Of course, Drew Stilton was the first name to appear in his team selection.

A team meeting with Jacky was scheduled for mid morning but, with the squad all assembled in the video room, in walked Joss Morecombe, smiling as usual with the assistant coach, Dave Geddis.

'I have a statement to read,' said Joss. 'And since the boss isn't here and Dave says he can't read, you're going to hear it from me. Before I say anything I want you to know that, whatever happens, Jacky has my full support and I hope that applies to everyone here, too.'

The players looked bemused and expectant and Joss began to read from a sheet of paper. ' "The Football Association has been informed by the Metropolitan Police that Mr Jack Dooley has been arrested on a charge of illegally accepting payments, and of failing to declare these payments to the Inland Revenue. Mr Dooley has appeared before magistrates at a preliminary hearing, and has been granted bail. Mr Dooley has informed the Football Association that he wishes to continue in his role as coach to the England World Cup side. The Football Association is taking all possible steps to ensure that these events do not affect the England team." ' Joss coughed and continued in his normal, less formal voice. 'Jacky's having a day off. He'll be back in the saddle tomorrow. Any questions?'

There was silence. 'What's going to happen then?' asked Jimmy Stinger at last. 'I mean, is he still in charge?'

'As far as I'm concerned he is,' said Joss. 'Mind you those back-stabbing politicians at the FA haven't exactly given him a vote of confidence. They're sitting on the fence, hedging their bets as usual.'

'Maybe he should step down,' said a voice at the back. Thomas recognised Drew Stilton's shrill tones. 'Let's have someone who can concentrate on running the side. His mind isn't on it any more.'

'Rubbish,' growled Joss, before anyone else could comment. 'Get one thing straight, laddie – nobody is going to replace Jacky Dooley. There isn't a man in the coaching set-up who wants him to go. And I'd better not hear another squeak out of you or you can get on your bike and pedal back to Sherwood sharpish. And one more thing – just in case you're in any doubt – Jacky Dooley is innocent and he'll be back in charge tomorrow.'

'And in the meantime we've got a training programme.' Dave Geddis spoke for the first time. 'So, if you want to have any chance of beating France, you'd better get out there.' The squad filed quietly out on to the practice ground.

Thomas noticed that Drew Stilton was even more sulky than usual in training. Drew had two moods, arrogant and morose, and he didn't know which to choose right now. Joss's words had got to him but the goal in the American game had pumped up his head. Thomas suspected that could only spell trouble. Drew Stilton thought he was the best, and if he didn't get picked for the French game – particularly with Ashleigh suspended – he wouldn't be at all easy to handle.

Selection for the game against France was no easy matter in any case. With Ashleigh and Rutherford Stacey out of the reckoning and Thomas, Rory Cameron, Jimmy Stinger and Dave Franchi on yellow cards, the boss had plenty of problems to add to his battle with the law.

The joint favourites to win the Cup were now Holland and Brazil, with Germany and France also fancied. England's stock with the press had now fallen to rock bottom. No one seemed to

think that they had even half a chance of qualifying for the knock-out stages any more and the
Group A position didn't look good because
France had beaten Nigeria 2–1. England's only
hope was to finish on five points behind France
– and that meant nothing but a victory would
do.

Group A

	P	W	L	D	F	A	Pts
France	2	2	0	0	3	1	6
England	2	0	0	2	5	5	2
Nigeria	2	0	1	1	5	6	1
United States	2	0	1	1	1	2	1

Norway led Group B and Germany had gone top
of Group C after a good 3–0 win against Spain but
the surprise result of the round was Portugal's
3–1 victory over Italy. Brazil had had a shock too
with Cameroon leading 2–0 at half time before the
champions finally ran out 3–2 victors.

Jacky Dooley kept a low profile for the next few
days. He made brief appearances at practice
sessions but he left most of the work to Dave
Geddis and Joss, and it was Dave who posted up
the team selected for the French game. There were
no big surprises – except perhaps for Drew
Stilton, who was on the bench along with Ally
Spink, Jason Le Braz, Ray Clooney and Marty
Mullett. The team was as follows:

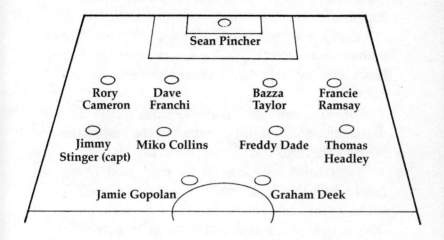

Sean Pincher

Rory Cameron   Dave Franchi   Bazza Taylor   Francie Ramsay

Jimmy Stinger (capt)   Miko Collins   Freddy Dade   Thomas Headley

Jamie Gopolan   Graham Deek

Drew didn't waste any time in putting his case. 'I want to complain to the boss,' he said to Dave. 'Where is he? Talking to his lawyers?'

Dave Geddis shrugged. 'He can't please every one, you know.'

'Yeah, but I'm not everyone. I'm the best striker in England. If you'd played me instead of Deek or Coltrane, we'd be at the top of our group right now.'

'Is that all you've got to say?' asked the assistant coach.

'No, it isn't,' said Drew. 'It's time I got my chance. Not just two minutes at the end of the game. And, what happens when I come on? You tell me.'

Dave shrugged. 'Good decision, then, wasn't it, super sub.'

'What's the problem?' asked Drew, his face taking on a nasty expression. 'Do I have to slip Jacky Dooley a fat wad of banknotes to get a game?'

'Get out, son,' said Dave Geddis softly. 'Say that again, and you'll be watching the rest of the World Cup from your living room armchair.'

'Don't think you can bully me,' said Drew, heading for the door. 'You just watch out, see?'

Drew missed the video session which Jacky Dooley and Joss Morecombe ran at 11 o'clock in the morning on the day before the French game. He said he had a migraine and stayed in his room.

The squad watched a re-run of the France–America game and also a France–Austria friendly which ended up 5–1 to the French. A hat trick by the young North African, Raoul Ramasseur, particularly impressed Thomas. He was a wispy, frail-looking figure, his head shaved except for a single brush of gold dyed hair just above his brow. His control and balance were perfect; he ghosted in and out of play in a way that made most of the opposition players look like old cart horses. All that and a devastating shot from both left and right foot, too.

'He wasn't brought on for the Nigeria game,' said Dooley, 'tummy trouble or something. But I hear he's back on the fit list now. If you ask me he's the biggest threat up front. So here's our plan. Bazza will mark Ramasseur with Francie dropping deeper to give a bit of extra cover. But everyone needs to tackle back. We can't afford to be caught on the hop by his pace.'

Thomas at last began to half understand why the best player in France, in his view, Paul Claudel – the St James United striker – had failed to get into the French squad. Part of the trouble was a row between Claudel and the French manager Jojo Berclé. But Jojo had so much young talent at his disposal with Ramasseur and the midfield trio of Cézanne Jacques, Michel Aubrais and Jacques Hareng, that he could almost afford to leave out Claudel. The St James forward was covering the World Cup for French Television, making star appearances and cashing in on advertising contracts everywhere. He seemed to be enjoying himself, although Thomas knew he'd have given up all the media stuff in a flash for a chance to play for his country.

The video session was drawing to a close when Dave Geddis appeared with a copy of the morning's *Post*. 'Seen this?' he said to Jacky Dooley. The back page headline read: 'ENGLAND PLAYERS REVOLT'. Dave read out the first paragraph. ' "Several players in the England squad have taken an unofficial vote of no confidence in the England manager who is currently fighting corruption and tax evasion charges and awaiting an FA decision on his future. The players, whom reliable sources say include Drew Stilton of Sherwood Strikers, Marty Mullett of Barbican and reserve goalkeeper, Ally Spink of Danebridge Forest, all believe that Jacky Dooley should go." '

Marty Mullett and Ally Spink looked at each other. The eyes of the rest of the team were upon them.

'First I've heard of it,' said Marty.

'News to me too,' said Ally. 'Either the *Post* is being wicked or someone's having us on.'

'And that someone isn't too far away if my guess is right,' said Joss Morecombe. 'Let's see . . . you two are managed by Arun Canin, aren't you?' Ally and Marty nodded. 'And who's Drew Stilton's manager?' continued Joss. 'My guess is that young Drew has been telling Arun a few porkies and we all know how close Arun is to the *Post* – God bless him.'

'Stilton knows he's not allowed to talk to the press, so he gets his agent to do it,' said Dave Geddis.

'And, of course, he'll deny every word of it,' said Ashleigh Coltrane. 'Wait till I get hold of the little . . .'

'You leave that to me, Ashleigh,' said Jacky Dooley and he sighed. 'Some people never learn, do they?'

*

The final Group games in the World Cup were now coming to a close. England were to play at the Cockpit the next day but most of the other quarter-finalists were already decided. As expected, Brazil and Holland won their groups comfortably. Scotland finished on four points after beating Japan but losing in extra time to Cameroon – four points wasn't enough to qualify. Argentina sneaked ahead of Norway on goal difference and Germany topped Group C in spite of an uninspiring 2–2 draw with South Africa. The other big surprise was Portugal pushing Italy into second place in Group E, although Italy with five points were still likely to qualify as one of the two leading runners-up.

The Cockpit was a complete sell-out, of course. Tickets were reported to be trading for £500 on the black market, even though only an England victory would take them and their supporters through to the last eight. The odds against them pulling that off had stretched to 4 to 1 against in the wake of the 'players revolt' story. The management had said nothing to Drew Stilton about it and Drew had kept himself to himself since the story appeared. None of the the other papers picked up on it and it was clear that Jacky Dooley's tactic was to ignore the *Post* and hope the nasty rumour would go away.

The weather forecast for the game was not good: westerly winds and showers.

'Suits me,' said Joss Morecombe cheerfully, as they sat in the coach on their way to the White Hart United ground and watched streaks of rain running down the windows. 'English weather. At least someone's on our side.'

7
ALLEZ LES BLEUS

The white shirts of England were defending the goal into which the rain lashed throughout the first half. And it wasn't just the rain that kept up a constant assault on the English. The blue-shirted French came at them in wave after wave.

With confidence high after their recent performances the French midfield dominated the first 45 minutes. They had more than 60% of the possession and only a heroic performance by Sean Pincher in goal and Bazza Taylor and Dave Franchi, who towered above the rest of the defence, prevented a landslide. Thomas, forced back deep into his own half, was alarmed at the freedom which the opposition's front runners had to penetrate the English back row. Jacky's 4–4–2 plan wasn't working and Thomas thought he knew why.

Sean Pincher

Rory Cameron   Dave Franchi   Bazza Taylor   Francie Ramsay

Jimmy Stringer   Miko Collins   Freddy Dade   Thomas Headley
(capt)   Jamie Gopolan   Graham Deek

Alexandre Salteau   Raoul Rammasseur

Cézanne Jacques   Michel Aubrais

Jean Chevalier   Henri Ecosse   Jacques Hareng   Kevin Moulins-Rives

Robbo Sabattier   Franc Elliaut

Guillaume Bâ (goal)

The French were playing what they termed 'le
tube'. It meant that eight players held the centre of
the park, moving up and back and interchanging
roles, while the wing backs, Chevalier and
Moulins-Rives, were free to ply the flanks – moving
up and down with electrifying pace and disrupting
the rigid English one-on-one marking. It took enormous effort and strength, but the two wingers were
super-fit. The English defenders, particularly Rory
and Francie, were having difficulties knowing
whom to mark and it was a typical wing movement
by Chevalier which left Salteau and then
Rammasseur loose in the centre. The ball fell to the
little genius's left foot and a searing drive buried
itself in the net, way beyond Sean's reach.

England were almost relieved to be only a goal down at half time. Jacky rearranged the formation into a 5–3–1–1 shape with Miko Collins dropping back and Bazza Taylor taking on a roving sweeper role to try and counter the threat of the two French forwards. But the manager knew they were still vulnerable out on the wings and, if Thomas and Jimmy Stinger were pulled out too wide, there would be gaping holes down the middle.

The second 45 minutes began as though the story of the first half was to be continued. Five minutes from the re-start Rammasseur put France further ahead with a brilliant curving shot from a set piece and it looked as though England had waved goodbye to any further progress in the World Cup. The chances of stealing three goals back against such mighty opposition were very remote. Some of the fans thought so and jeers and chants rang out from the section of the crowd behind the dugout. The England skipper came in for the worst abuse.

'If Stinger plays for England so can I
If Stinger plays for England so can I
And so can Mickey Mouse and Sooty and
    Popeye!'

St James's supporters, thought Thomas. The St James's fans had hated Jimmy Stinger since he'd transferred from St James to Highfield Rovers, particularly as Rovers had just beaten them in the Premiership.

But within a minute England were back in touch again and Jimmy had answered his critics in the best possible way. His forceful run pulled the play over to the right. Then he found Thomas with a magnificent long ball to the far wing. Thomas went outside his marker, took it on to the goal line and whipped in a low cross which Freddy Dade met with a diving header. Bâ in the French goal could only flap at the ball and then slowly turn and pick it out of the back of the net.

'Cadastre,' swore the goalie. He booted the ball savagely up the pitch for the re-start and then kicked the goal post.

'Game on,' said Deekie as the English celebrations came to an end.

'All or nothing,' agreed Thomas.

'We've got to keep running at them, pressurising them,' said Jimmy Stinger, gathering his forwards round him. 'Their man-to-man marking doesn't give us a lot of space. But take your marker on and that gives us a man over. We'll hit them on the outside. Get the ball out to me or Thomas.'

An injury to Jamie Gopolan after a crunching tackle by the Blues' hard man, Franc Elliaut, brought on Drew Stilton with 15 minutes of the game to run. Drew strutted about a bit and then he too was brought down by Elliaut. 'Mains propres!' shrugged the French full back looking the picture of innocence. Drew went to retaliate and the Frenchman stood his ground with a smile as if daring Stilton to hit him. Jimmy Stinger pulled Drew away just in time.

'Listen, laddie. You get sent off and you're finished for ever as an England player. Last warning. Not another word, okay?'

Drew scowled but said nothing.

With time running out the crowd was at last giving England some real support. Now the white shirts were surging forward – and, if they weren't quite as fluent as the French in attack, there was no lack of passion. Deekie went close with a header and then Drew hit the crossbar with a fierce right-footed drive. The attacks became more and more desperate and the French held out. Ten minutes to go – it was going to take something special to keep England in the Cup.

Thomas tackled back and won the ball from Aubrais, the French captain. A one-two with Freddy Dade gave him space on the left again and, with the roar of the crowd giving him fresh legs, he powered down the wing. Suddenly he caught sight of Drew Stilton on the far post and curled the perfect ball behind the defence into his path. Drew, for once, didn't go for glory but stabbed a pass back to Graham Deek, running inside him. Deekie hardly broke his stride. The left-foot shot had the net bulging before Bâ could move.

'Allez les Bleus
Allez back to France
When we've hammered you
We'll do the World Cup dance.'

The World Cup dance was a sort of fans' imitation of the Coltrane shuffle – Ashleigh's famous limbo jig with which he celebrated all his goals. The England supporters had taken it up and one whole side of the Cockpit terraces bobbed up and down in unison as they sang.

The surly Bâ wasn't amused. 'Villeins regardants,' he snarled at his defenders.

With the score at 2–2, the game took on a passion and frenzy which had the entire crowd on their feet. 'Oooooh!' they went as a header from Salteau was touched over by Sean Pincher. 'OOOOOOOH!' again as Freddy Dade slid into the box and just failed to reach a low cross from the right wing. The game went into stoppage time. Four minutes was signalled by an official from the touchline.

Jacky Dooley sat motionless in the dug-out, his face showing no emotion. 'I'm not making another substitution,' he said quietly to Joss Morecombe alongside him. 'The lads are running at them with passion. It's up to them now.'

Joss nodded in approval.

The French, however, brought on two substitutes in midfield who tested the legs of the

England back row. Thomas tangled with Franc Elliaut who pushed him as he was going down the wing. Minutes later the little French terrier ran at Thomas with the ball and deliberately dived as Thomas closed in for the tackle. There had been no contact but the ref was fooled and the linesman unsighted. Elliaut said something incomprehensible in French which sounded like 'pan fort et dur' – probably French for hard cheese thought Thomas as he coldly refused Elliaut's cynical offer of a handshake and then the inevitable yellow card appeared. Thomas put his head down and walked away. But a feeling of grim determination rose within him.

France continued to attack and then defend in numbers. They were incredibly fit. A fierce drive on goal was brilliantly parried round the post by Sean who was having a dream game; the corner brought another stunning save from him and a round of applause from the fans. But everyone knew the ball needed to be at the other end. The seconds ticked by. Sean's throw fell to the feet of Dade who slotted a quick throughball to Deekie – he'd moved a little wider on the left and Thomas took the opportunity to come inside, taking his marker with him. Deekie back-heeled to Drew Stilton who had followed him across and the Strikers forward knocked the ball instantly to Thomas. As it hit his chest Thomas turned and the movement took him past Hareng at his shoulder and into the path of Elliaut who immediately came in two-footed at the ball and at Thomas's ankles. A deft jink to the left and a hop over the flying tackle put Thomas in the clear. As he landed he struck the ball with his left foot and it powered to the right of Bâ who got his fingers to it but couldn't keep the shot out. He pummelled the ground with his fist, but it was too late. England had come back from the dead.

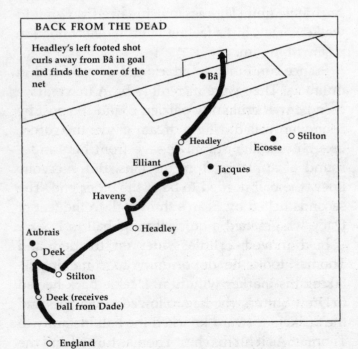

BACK FROM THE DEAD

Headley's left footed shot curls away from Bâ in goal and finds the corner of the net

Bâ

Headley
Stilton
Ecosse
Elliant
Jacques
Haveng
Headley
Aubrais
Deek
Stilton
Deek (receives ball from Dade)

○ England
● France

The crowd rose as one and the deafening roar brought the match to an end. No one heard the ref's whistle blow for full time. Thomas was lying flat on his back, buried under the bodies of his team-mates. Three–two. It was the greatest escape since World War II. They had beaten the mighty French team. They were through to the knock-outs. But as Thomas lay there – relieved and jubilant – he couldn't forget that yellow card. It ruled him out of the next game.

A cynical dive and a poor refereeing decision had denied him a game in the quarter-finals of the World Cup.

There was a big outcry in the press the next morning about Thomas's suspension. Diabolical, Katie Moncrieff called it in the *Mirror*. But it made no difference – Thomas missed a game.

Katie rang Thomas to commiserate with him over the verdict as well as to congratulate him on his goal.

'It's disgraceful,' she said. 'That ref could have cost you Player of the Tournament and without you in the side, England's chances of getting past Argentina are probably halved.'

'That's a bit harsh on the other guys,' said Thomas.

'Maybe. But who else have we got who can play down the left? Freddy Dade, perhaps – but he's better on his right foot and he is not half as strong tackling back as you are. Without you the whole team loses its balance.'

Thomas smiled to himself and said nothing. 'Sorry about Scotland,' he said to change the subject and hide his embarrassment. 'They were unlucky. That goal was well offside.'

The brave battle of the Scottish team to get to the quarter-finals had foundered on a disputed golden goal against Cameroon.

'I feel sorry for Jamie MacLachlan, he played his heart out.'

'Best player in the country,' agreed Thomas. He was about to put the phone down when Katie spoke again.

'One other thing, Thomas,' he heard her say. 'You know that Club Strikers restaurant chain that you and the boys were thinking of investing in.'

'Yeah.'

'Well, don't.'

'Why not?'

'Because I've heard it's a scam. Arun Canin's been sucked in by a bunch of crooks. There are no sites, no planning permission, just a collection of half-baked plans and shiny prospectuses. I'm not sure whether it's Canin who's bent or his business partners. But I'd keep well clear of it.'

'Too late,' mumbled Thomas.

'What?'

'I said, too late. I've already invested. So have Rory and Jason and Drew. One or two of the others are keen, too.'

'How much have you . . .'

'Fifty grand.'

'What! You must be mad. That's far more than I earn in a year.'

Thomas was silent. He didn't like the idea of losing all that money. But he specially didn't like the idea of Arun Canin, slimy Stilton's smart agent, making a fool of him.

Katie spoke again. 'Listen, don't worry. I'll talk to Elaine about it. She'll know how to handle it.'

'But she doesn't know that I've . . .'

'You haven't told her? Hell, Thomas. Don't you think you should? Oh forget it. The last thing you should be doing is worrying about money. I'll talk to her. Are you going to the game on Tuesday?'

'Of course. I'll be with the squad. I only wish I was playing.'

'Maybe see you there then. Bye.'

Thomas switched off his mobile. He wondered whether he should talk to Drew Stilton about the Club Strikers business. Arun Canin must have told him all about it. But could he bear to talk to Drew? He was such a creep.

The draw for the quarter-finals brought England up against their old World Cup foe, Argentina. The games were as follows:

England v Argentina	Wembley	Tuesday 3 pm
Germany v Brazil	City Ground	Tuesday 7 pm
Portugal v Holland	Stadium of the North	Wednesday 3 pm
France v Italy	Kings Road	Wednesday 7 pm

With Rutherford Stacey nursing a groin injury, Ray Clooney suffering from food poisoning and Ashleigh and Thomas suspended, the original England squad of 22 was now reduced to 16 with the quarter-final game pending – and three of those were goalies.

Because of the need to prepare the team for a new formation, Jacky Dooley had a long session talking with Joss Morecombe and Dave Geddis and then took the unusual step of announcing his team selection four days before the game – telling everyone to keep it well under wraps and away from the press and the Argentinian spies.

Reserves: Ally Spink, Marty Mullett, Drew Stilton, Henderson Springer.

It was a 4–4–2 formation with a difference. Jason Le Braz came in as a wing back which allowed Jimmy Stinger and Jamie Gopolan to switch wings from time to time. The availability of cover was vital – which meant careful and painstaking practising of a range of build-ups and an equal number of plans for defence when the attacks broke down. The idea was to stretch the Argentinian midfield to breaking point and Jacky had decided that variety was the key to combating the Argentinian system. To be honest, he didn't have many other options. The one problem, as Joss had warned him, was Drew Stilton. With only three reserves available Drew knew how much the manager needed him – even if he hadn't picked him to start the game. That meant he could afford to be even more difficult than usual about not being an automatic starting choice, especially after playing so well again as sub in the French game. Drew wasn't one to miss out on an opportunity to be difficult. He moaned and complained to anyone who would listen – although most of the team chose to ignore him.

So when Thomas chose his moment to ask Drew about Club Striker, the anger and resentment came to the surface.

'What are you saying, Headley, that my manager's a crook?'

'No, I just wanted to know why . . .'

'You're just lucky to be allowed in on this. But

if you want out, I'll ring him now and tell him what a white-livered creep you are. He'll listen to me. Want your money back, do you?'

Thomas swallowed hard. 'Well, I've just heard that Mr Canin is . . .'

'At least I'm not managed by my mother. What did Mummy say? "Don't you risk your precious money with that nasty Arun Canin. He'll just run away with it. Give it to Mummy." '

'Don't be stupid, Drew.'

'Stupid? Me? I'll tell you who's stupid. Dooley and Morecombe are stupid for not picking the best striker in the country; Jimmy Stinger's stupid for not standing up to them and being a feeble captain; Jason Le Braz is stupid and a one-legged footballing dwarf and you're just stupid. Pig stupid.'

As Drew pushed his face closer Thomas realized he'd been drinking heavily. He looked hard at Drew, shrugged his shoulders and turned to walk away. But Drew caught him by the arm and, as he pulled him round, he threw a punch which caught Thomas on the side of the head. Thomas pushed him away hard and his attacker fell over on his back with a thump. Roaring with fury now Drew leapt up and dived at Thomas. His head caught Thomas in the solar plexus and they fell to the floor together. Thomas was completely winded. He was struggling to free himself after getting an elbow in the eye when he saw Dave Geddis standing over him.

'Get up, you two,' said Dave. 'You're pathetic. More like a pair of kids. Get up and come with me. This is one for the manager to sort out. My God, call yourselves professionals?'

8
SIDELINED

Life just isn't fair, thought Thomas Headley. Everything had been going so well and now, through no fault of his own, here he was – banned from the next game in the World Cup, and, after the punch-up with Drew Stilton, in deep trouble with the national coach and the FA.

Drew Stilton, first to be interviewed by Jack Dooley, had already packed his bags and left Chiving Beacon that morning, his face pale, saying nothing. His dismissal from the England team had been instant. Jacky didn't even want to know Drew's side of the story – he'd had enough. Thomas had to wait until the afternoon for his disciplinary interview. It had been postponed from the morning because Jacky was too busy to see him. Miserably he sat in the lounge outside the manager's suite at Chiving Beacon. The rest of the England players were out training and he had only himself for company.

His mobile phone buzzed and he took it out, planning not to answer. Then he looked at the caller check and saw it was Elaine. He growled a hello.

'Thomas?' There was an anxious note in his mother's voice. 'I've just been talking to Joss Morecombe. He told me what happened yesterday – about Drew Stilton.'

'Yeah. Drew's been kicked out.'

'I know. I asked Joss what would happen to you, but he didn't know. He said it's up to Jack Dooley and he can't interfere. You didn't start it, did you, Thomas?'

'No. I wasn't fighting at all – just holding him off.'

'I was sure you didn't . . . Well, we must just hope he'll be fair. Poor man, he has troubles of his own. Joss said your interview was put off because the police came to see him again this morning. You must ring me as soon as you come out. Promise?'

'Okay.'

'And remember, I believe in you.'

'Thanks, Elaine.' For the first time, there was some warmth in Thomas's reply.

But when he clicked the phone off, gloom set in again. Realising that his team-mates would soon be coming in for lunch, he went up to his room. The first thing he saw was the shiny prospectus for Club Striker Restaurants. Angrily, he screwed it up and dropped it in the waste-paper basket. Then he slumped on his bed and gazed blankly at the ceiling.

The other members of the England squad weren't much more cheerful. The sacking of Drew had been a shock, even though the arrogant striker had few friends in the squad.

'What d'you reckon Tommo's chances are?' Jason asked Ashleigh.

'I don't know. Not too good, I guess.'

'We can't lose Headley. The squad would be down to 18 and we'd be completely dead in midfield,' said Francie Ramsay.

'We're gonna have to manage without him tomorrow,' said Rory Cameron. 'My money's on him being out for the tournament.'

'Mine too,' said Freddy Dade. 'If they've chucked Cheesy out they'll probably feel they've got to sack Thomas too. Even though it wasn't his fault, everyone knows he hates Drew's guts.'

Only the skipper, Jimmy Stringer, kept his views to himself. He was a big fan of Thomas Headley but even he wasn't sure how Jacky Dooley would react. The two men hadn't spoken about it although Jacky had asked his team captain to be present at the interview. So at five to three Jimmy knocked on Thomas's door. Thomas opened it and stared at him without saying a word.

'Ready?' said Jimmy.

' 'Spose so.'

'Just one thing. Don't try to tough it out. Act sorry. You flaming well should be sorry anyway.'

Thomas's heart was beating as fast as it ever had on the football field as they entered the manager's office. Jack Dooley was there, with Dave Geddis and two senior FA officials whom Thomas had seen before but never spoken to. Their faces looked cold and forbidding. He had hoped Joss Morecombe would be present but there was no sign of the Strikers manager.

In a toneless voice, Dave Geddis reported the fight and how he had broken it up. 'The other person involved was clearly the worse for drink, but Headley here appeared to be sober,' added Geddis.

'What have you to say?' asked Jacky Dooley.

'I'm very sorry,' said Thomas. 'It was stupid. I let myself be provoked. I shouldn't have done it.'

'I believe that's true,' said Geddis. 'About being provoked. I spoke to two of the players who saw something of it and they say Headley did not start it.'

'Nevertheless, he responded. He could have walked away,' drawled one of the hard-faced FA men.

'How could I when –' Thomas began hotly. Then he remembered the skipper's advice. 'I should have walked away,' he said quietly.

He was sent to wait in a bare ante-room, then summoned back after a wait of 15 minutes which seemed more like 15 hours. Jack Dooley's face was severe; he feared the worst.

'We are determined to take whatever action is necessary to safeguard the reputation of the England side, on and off the pitch,' he said. 'Your foolish behaviour has done nothing to help that. The disciplinary committee must take a very serious view of such a clear breakdown of discipline . . .'

Oh, no, thought Thomas.

'. . . and the other person involved, as you know, has been dismissed from the squad. Taking into account all the circumstances, we have decided not to take the same course of action with you, but to give you a severe warning and caution. You will be fined £8,000 from your match fees and any further breach of team discipline is likely to end in your departure from the England side. Is that understood?'

'Yes,' said Thomas. He felt like smiling but he managed to keep a serious expression on his face. He was still in the squad. That was what mattered.

A short statement was read out by the England manager to the awaiting press:

'Following a serious breach of discipline after a training session, Drew Stilton has been removed from the England World Cup squad. Thomas Headley has received a fine of £8,000 and a formal warning from the England manager. The incident is now closed.'

The questions which followed from the packed press room indicated that, as far as they were concerned the matter was far from closed. As one of the reporters said, 'This is beginning to look like the most accident-prone England team in the history of the game.'

Thomas sat alongside Ashleigh Coltrane in a packed Wembley Stadium watching the England–Argentina game. They were both on the edge of their seats throughout a hard fought first half. The action was mostly in the centre of the pitch with neither goalkeeper having a lot to do. The battle for midfield supremacy swayed first one way, then the other. It was 0–0 at half time but Thomas thought, on the balance of play, that the Argentinians had controlled more of the action. They'd certainly had most of the possession. Graham Deek and Freddie Dade had failed to get into the game and the marking of Rivada and Blanco left them little room for manoeuvre.

After the interval the game opened up a little.

The Argentines won a couple of corners and Freddy Dade had a shot on target at the other end.

'Come on, come on,' muttered Ashleigh in frustration as Miko Collins chested down a long kick from Sean Pincher, turned, and hesitated while Graham Deek and Freddy Dade raced ahead of him. Collins went down to a heavy tackle from behind and the ball bounced away into the path of Jimmy Stinger. The referee waved advantage. Jimmy sensed Jason Le Braz to his right and curved a pass out to the wing. Jason, who had been having a hard game of it in defence, finally got his chance to move up field. He took the ball and raced up the flank, went round his marker, just avoided putting the ball out of play and crossed perfectly. Deekie's header was parried by the keeper and half cleared out to Freddy Dade. Seeing himself blocked, Dade found Jason again on the right. Jason, who had crept inside, dummied his marker and fired in a fierce shot from 15 yards past Borges, the Argentinian goalie.

Argentina 0–England 1

Thomas and Ashleigh danced in each other's arms as the crowd roared with delight.

'Jason Le Braz, you are beautiful,' sang Ashleigh. 'It had to be a Striker.'

The crowd went silent again as Blanco peeled off in a in a curving run after the re-start. He tapped the ball back to Rivada, coming in unmarked, and received a pass to run onto. With an open view of the goal, he blasted it towards the top corner. The shot seemed unstoppable. But, somehow, Pincher got his fingertips to it, deflecting the ball just enough for it to glance away harmlessly off the top of the bar. The England supporters cheered again, and Thomas grinned as he saw the goalie draw his finger across his bushy moustache, as he always did when he pulled off a special save.

'It had to be a Striker,' he said to Ashleigh, with a smile.

From then on it was non-stop and no game for the faint-hearted. The Argentinians piled on the pressure. Thomas and Ashleigh were out of their seats a hundred times as the play surged backwards and forwards. When the final whistle sounded Ashleigh fell to his knees. 'Am I glad I'm a player,' he said. 'I can't bear the excitement of watching. I don't think my nerves could stand being an England supporter again.'

'Maybe we won't be watching, next time,' said Thomas.

'Don't be too sure. There wasn't a player out there who didn't give everything. Jacky will have a hard job telling any of them that they're not needed in the semi-final.'

Semi-final, thought Thomas. Only one team separated England from their first appearance in a World Cup final since 1966. Who would it be, he wondered.

Italy? Or would they have to play France again?

9
BLUFF AND COUNTER-BLUFF

The excitement of the game had taken Thomas's mind off an unpleasant letter which he had received on the morning of the game. It was headed Canin Investments.

Dear Mr Headley,
Thank you for your letter indicating that you wish to withdraw from your investment in Club Striker Restaurants. I regret to tell you this is quite impossible. You have signed a formal and irrevocable contract to invest £50,000 and if you fail to do submit your funds, we shall be obliged to instigate legal proceedings against you to obtain the money due to us.
Yours sincerely,
A. Canin

As Thomas reread the letter, he thought about Elaine. He should have explained things to her earlier, he knew that. But now – somehow he didn't want to talk about it. It could wait until after the World Cup, he thought. Perhaps Arun Canin would change his mind – although the things he'd learned about him so far didn't fill him with optimism on that score.

What Thomas didn't know was that as he stared at the letter something very significant was taking place at his home in Sherwood. There had been some strange visitors to the Headley household but Arun Canin was definitely one of the oddest. Elaine told Thomas afterwards that he looked like a little fat rock fish in a camel-hair overcoat. Small and fat, he had popping eyes and not much chin. But there was determination in the little man – Elaine sensed that straightaway.

'I'll come straight to the point, Mrs Headley,' he said as he sipped his coffee. 'Your son entered into an agreement with me to invest in Club Striker. It's too late now to back out. That's perfectly clear.'

'So you say, Mr Canin,' said Elaine quietly. She had invited Arun Canin to discuss the investment with her and she was determined to remain polite and courteous, whatever happened.

'And I can't honestly see the problem,' continued Arun Canin. 'It's a wonderful opportunity.

You must appreciate that. I believe you were in restaurant management yourself.'

'You're very well informed, Mr Canin. So perhaps you'll show me where the restaurants are going to be built. What are the precise locations?'

Mr Canin waved a hand. 'Of course we don't have all the sites yet. But we know where we want to be. Believe me, I'm working night and day to ensure your son's investment will make a very big profit, Mrs Headley. A very big profit indeed.'

'Well I'm acting on behalf of Thomas – and his friends Rory Betts and Jason Le Braz,' continued Elaine. 'And I can assure you that all three of them are withdrawing from your scheme.'

'Impossible,' said Mr Canin, flatly. 'What's more, your son's payment is well overdue. I want my money now.'

'Can I ask you one question, Mr Canin?' said Elaine, softly.

'Sure. Ask away.'

'Are you the Mr Arun Canin who was managing director of SuperStar Properties?'

Mr Canin's expression changed. He looked surprised, and angry. 'What if I was?'

'If you are, Mr Canin,' said Elaine, 'you are disqualified from running any company in this country. SuperStar Properties went bust owing £20 million, and you were the managing director and major shareholder. A lot of people lost a lot of money, and you were barred from being a company director for five years, I believe. Lucky not to go to prison, if you ask me. But the point is that you still have two years to go of your disqualification, Mr Canin.'

There was a silence. Mr Canin's popping eyes seemed to leap even further out of his head. 'Well,' he said at last, 'if you want to rake up old history, there's no point in my staying. It's all complete slander, of course. Not a word of truth in it. You'll be hearing from my lawyers.' He turned to leave.

'I doubt it,' said Elaine pleasantly. 'Naturally I've recorded this conversation and, if we hear any more from you, I'll be sending the tape to Katie Moncrieff at the *Mirror*, who was good enough to uncover this information for me in the first place. I assume you want to stay in football management. Well, I can promise you that Katie and I will make quite sure you don't if you pursue your Club Striker enterprise.'

Arun Canin stood up. His mouth opened and closed and then he buttoned up his coat and walked to the door. 'I won't forget this,' he muttered as Elaine opened to door for him to leave. She smiled to herself and then picked up the phone and dialled Katie Moncrieff's mobile.

*

England 1   Argentina 0
Germany 1   Brazil 2
Portugal 2   Holland 2 (Holland won 5–3 on penalties)
France 2   Italy 3 (Italy scored the golden goal in extra time)

The semi-finals of the World Cup would be fought out between England and Italy and Holland and the world champions, Brazil. Brazil were still favourites to win the Cup but after Holland's displays in the tournament so far, the England camp were pleased not to be meeting either of them in the semi-final.

'Not that Italy's going to be exactly a pushover,' said Jason.

'We can do it,' said Thomas.

His confidence took a jolt on the day before the game though, when Ashleigh Coltrane fell in training and damaged his right arm. He also appeared to have fractured a finger. It was a terrible blow to an already depleted side and cruel luck too. Ashleigh's unjustified suspension was over and he had been looking sharp in practice. He was such a key player in the England set-up and no other striker had his depth of experience. Jacky Dooley only option was to draft Jamie Gopolan into the front row. The line-up for England was:

Sean Pincher

Jason Le Braz   Dave Franchi   Bazza Taylor   Francie Ramsay

Jimmy Stinger (capt)   Rory Cameron   Miko Collins   Thomas Headley

Freddy Dade   Graham Deek

Reserves: Ally Spink, Marty Mullett, Jamie Gopolan, Henderson Springer.

Facing them were:

Gian Gubbio

Marco Castiglione   Franco Cesario   Giorgio Raffaelo   Lucco Grimaldi

Cosimo Lagattello   Sergio Gambolini   Stefan Di Fano (capt)

Cristo Stanislas   Dino Malpiero   Toni Mirandola

The Italian manager had stuck to his fluid 4–3–3 formation throughout the competition. In midfield the Strikers' pairing of Lagattello and Gambolini had been brilliant throughout. Thomas exchanged a wink before the kick-off with his Strikers team-mate, Cozzie Lagattello. Nicknamed 'Pasta' by the Strikers fans, it looked as if the Italian had been training seriously: his waistline was distinctly more streamlined than it had been at the end of the Premiership season. He was one of the most experienced players in an Italian side whose average age was almost five years older than the England team. They knew every trick in the book, and more. Only Pincher, Stinger, Taylor and Franchi in the England side were over twenty-five.

The referee, a bearded German, got the game away to a prompt start. The Italians took the kick-off and instantly put pressure on the English back row. Malpiero and Stanislas were in partnership on the right, the Italian crowd's favourite, Mirandola, was on the left and their skipper Di Fano had the job of controlling things with Lagattello and Gambolini in the centre of the park. England found themselves pushed back and compressed in their own half.

Thomas discovered that, wherever he went, the lean and powerful shape of Castiglione was right by him. He had rarely been marked quite so closely, and he saw the same thing happening to the other players, particularly the two strikers – they simply had no room to manoeuvre.

The log jam continued until five minutes before half time. Thomas noticed Jimmy Stinger having a word with Deekie – and he soon saw what it was they had been talking about. From an England goal kick, Jimmy pounced on the ball and sent a route one clearance up-field in the path of Graham Deek. His perfectly timed sprint had left him just onside and he reached the ball a yard clear of the nearest defender. The shot was perfect, low and swerving, and the keeper was well beaten. Two minutes later the Stinger/Deek combination opened up the Italian defence again. This time Deekie went for the near post and his shot was every bit as deadly. Then, on the stroke of half time, the Italians got one back with a goal hammered in at short range by Mirandola. Five crazy minutes had transformed the game. At half time it was 2–1 to England.

Jacky Dooley was pleased with the first half performance but Thomas and the other midfielders had had a frustrating time of it, closed down by the intense marking of the Italians. Now they were ahead it was their turn to frustrate the opposition. It's going to be a rough old second half, Thomas thought.

A goal down, the Italians came powering back at the beginning of the second half just as they had done at the start of the game. In the press of players converging on goal the referee and his linesmen had a difficult job seeing what was going on. Once Thomas saw Dave Franchi appear to control the ball with his hand as Malpiero came running in to tackle. The Italian screamed in protest, but none of the officials had seen the incident and Dave nonchalantly tapped the ball into touch. Thomas imagined the continual TV replays of the incident as the Italians surrounded the ref, waving their arms and fruitlessly demanding a penalty.

Jamie Gopolan came on for Miko Collins who had sustained a nasty knock on the knee, and 15 minutes into the second half, as Deek and Gopolan were again racing onto a throughball from Jimmy Stinger, there was a moment which the pundits were to argue about for weeks to come. Deekie controlled the throughball and as he was tackled he fed it inside to Jamie Gopolan. Across came the full back, Cesario, who tackled Jamie from the side. The Italian missed the ball and Jamie went down inside the area, rolling over and over. 'PENALTY!' screamed the crowd. As the ref blew his whistle, the assistant ref ran onto the pitch and the two of them held a brief conversation with the assistant referee pointing accusingly at Jamie. The referee beckoned to Jamie and held up a yellow card. Jamie was outraged and he showed it. Before Jimmy Stinger could race up and intervene, Jamie must have said something to the ref who immediately pulled out the red card and gesticulated to the touchline. The fans howled with rage. It had looked like a foul by the Italian but Jamie had been penalised for diving. And the protests of the England team made no difference to the German ref. Six minutes later, in another borderline decision, the referee gave a penalty against England, after Dave Franchi and Malpiero appeared to go for a 50-50 ball. Malpiero put on a fine performance as he hit the deck and got the decision. Malpiero took the kick himself and sent Sean Pincher the wrong way. It was level-pegging.

The England ten struggled on to full time with the crowd cheering their every move and booing the ref and Malpiero unmercifully. In extra time they took everything the Italians could throw at them and very nearly sneaked the golden goal when Deekie cracked in a surprise shot from the edge of the area. Gubbio in the Italian goal got down quickly to deny him his hat trick. It remained 2–2 and in the end the penalty shoot-out seemed inevitable.

Joss Morecombe had made a big thing about everyone practising penalties and four of England's top penalty takers were on the pitch: Deek, Headley, Stinger and Franchi. But who would replace Ashleigh Coltrane? Thomas Headley was relieved to be chosen as the first England player to shoot.

The Italians won the call of the coin and Sean Pincher patted his fingertips together and crouched, facing Malpiero again. In a replica of the equalizer, the Italian sent the ball flying past him as Sean dived in the other direction.

Now it was Thomas's turn. He had not forgotten the terrible moment in Rome when he'd missed – and lost Strikers their chance of winning the UEFA Cup. He felt that old wound heal at last, as the ball left his foot, flew low past Gubbio, and punched out the net. One–One.

The stadium was quiet. In millions of homes the atmosphere was equally tense. Lagattello was next, and came running in at an angle. Pincher was fooled and wrong-footed, and Cozzie ran away with his hands in the air. But a calm Jimmy Stinger equalised again with one of the most powerful place kicks Thomas had ever seen. The ball seemed to explode into the net, and the England supporters rose with frenzied cheers. Sean pulled off a brilliant one-handed save to deny Stanislas, only to watch the Italian goalie go one better and tip over Graham Deek's drive. Thomas put his arm around Deekie and tried to console him. He knew how he felt.

Then Mirandola scored for Italy. Up ran Dave Franchi and sidestepped the ball low to Gubbio's left, making it 3–3. Sudden death was approaching. Like a true captain Di Fano stepped up to take responsibility. He placed the ball with lingering care, walked slowly back and then attacked it. It was a fine shot, fast, low, heading straight for the corner of the net. But Pincher launched himself at it, full stretch, and thrust it away just as it was about to dip under the bar. Thomas heard the Italians groan. Freddy Dade was the coach's choice as the fifth penalty taker. In spite of his youth he had plenty of experience of taking spot kicks with Highfield Rovers where he shared the responsibility with Graham Deek. Freddy prepared himself. Thomas closed his eyes. He couldn't look. But he sensed from the gasp of the crowd that Freddy was on the point of launching his shot and he forced himself to peep at the last moment. For a split second it seemed Freddy had hit it too high but the ball grazed the under-side of the crossbar and went in. Brilliant!

England were through to the final.

10
DUTCH TREAT

Holland beat Brazil 3–2 after extra time. It was an extraordinary game – the best of the tournament, the press said – full of wonderful flowing football and brilliant defending. Brazil were leading 2–1 until the 94th minute of play when a thunderbolt of a shot from man of the match, Rudi Kraal, brought the scores level. The golden goal was scored by Kraal too after the Dutch had withstood an unbelievable 25 minutes of pressure from Brazil in extra time. There were few weaknesses in this remarkable Dutch side. If England were going to beat them they would have to play their best football of the tournament, and then some.

The next four days were a blur in the life of Thomas Headley. After it was all over he tried to remember some of the things he had done or seen or heard during that extraordinary time, but he could think of virtually nothing until the very morning of the final itself. And what a day that was!

Jacky Dooley had imposed what he called 'a complete communications blackout' on the 19 players who made up the depleted England squad. That meant not only no talking to the press, but no newspapers and no phone calls. Married players were permitted one call a day to their wives and kids but that was all. Radio and TV were allowed, but in reality most of the players spent their time, in between sleep and training sessions, watching videos, reading or, in the case of Miko Collins and Bazza Taylor, betting on the horses with the assistance of one of the Irish waiters in the Chiving Beacon restaurant. Ashleigh Coltrane was rarely seen without his Walkman and a lot of card and computer games were played, too.

The injury and suspension picture was pretty bad. Ashleigh was determined to play in the final in spite of his damaged arm and finger, which were heavily strapped, but Miko Collins's knee was still giving him a lot of pain and, of course, Jamie Gopolan was out of the reckoning because of his sending off. No one blamed Jamie for the original mistake by the referee – he insisted he had been brought down and everyone believed him – but Jamie knew that his momentary loss of temper had cost him his rightful place in the final and he was completely gutted about that.

Joss and Jacky discussed the options left to them

and they both favoured a 4–3–3 line-up and a flat back four against the Dutch. Freddy Dade and Graham Deek would play just behind Ashleigh, leaving Jimmy and Thomas freer roles in midfield. The big gamble was playing Rory Cameron in an almost old fashioned centre-half-cum-sweeper role. It was a big part for him, particularly in the face of the Dutch midfield menace of Sorg, Trimbach and Gresser, but Rory had had a good World Cup and both managers had confidence in him. As least the back four were still intact. England's successes had depended so much on the 'thin white line' – especially big Dave Franchi and Bazza Taylor in the centre – and behind them the immense, towering presence of Sean Pincher in goal. This was the likely starting line-up for the World Cup final.

Reserves: Ally Spink, Marty Mullett, Henderson Springer, Rutherford Stacey, Ray Clooney.

On the morning of the final there was a knock
on the door of the room Thomas was sharing with
Graham Deek. Deekie had already gone down to
breakfast.

'Room service, sir,' said a voice.

Thomas opened the door and there stood Katie
Moncrieff.

'Wha' the . . .'

'Quick let me in before anyone spots me. And
no laughing at my outfit.' Katie was dressed as a
chamber-maid, complete with white pinafore. 'I
had to see you, Thomas. I've got a message from
Elaine. And I've got news about the manager,
too.'

'Jacky?'

'Yes. He's been exonerated.'

'What?'

'He's not guilty. The police have dropped all
charges. And there's a rumour that the *Post* is
going to get it in the neck for obstructing the
course of justice by making up false stories. I'd
sue them if I were Jacky.'

'Does Jacky know?'

'Yes. The police rang him this morning. That
should cheer him up. Good news for the final,
isn't it? And the other bit of excellent news is
that Elaine and I have saved you £50,000. That
Club Strikers deal was a big empty promise – I
did a bit of scratching around and I found out a
lot of interesting things about Mr Arun Canin.

I'll tell you all about him later. He needed the cash badly and he thought he'd got his corrupt little hands on your money and Jason's and Rory's. Well he was wrong – and you can tell Jason when you see him that we've saved him £50k too.'

Thomas didn't quite know what to say. He'd got himself into a fix and Katie and Elaine had got him out of it. He settled for, 'Thanks.'

'That's OK. Now all you've got to think about is winning the World Cup. How about a quote for the *Mirror*?'

Thomas grinned. 'Write what you like. You usually do.'

At last the great game that everyone had been talking about for months got underway. As expected, Thomas found himself closely shadowed by the Dutch master ballplayer, Piet Van Hoof. Van Hoof had been one of the stars of the Holland side for three or four years. He currently played for Real Madrid and his World Cup form had been outstanding. The Dutch moved the ball about beautifully, building slowly and then darting penetrative passes through the English defence. Possession is going to to be the key to this game, thought Thomas.

England had two chances to go ahead in the first quarter. After eight minutes Coltrane laid off

Stinger's long ball to Dade, striding through to his right, but Rolly Gassmann in the Holland goal, unorthodox as ever, managed to kick the shot away even though it had taken a deflection.

Just past the 20 minute mark Cameron wafted his shot over the bar after Coltrane had nodded on another ball from Stinger. Most of the England moves seemed to be coming down the right – mainly because Thomas and Francie Ramsay had their work cut out on the other flank to control the dangerous Holland combination of Van Hoof and Veenstra who pushed forward at every opportunity.

On the half hour the England defence was caught square when Van Hoof flicked on from De Caro and Rudi Kraal, sprinting through to beat Franchi to the ball, scored with an unstoppable drive to Pincher's left. Then just before half time an exchange of passes by Van Hoof and Veenstra on the right allowed Bruno Sorg to centre low for Kraal to run in again, in front of Taylor this time, and score at the near post.

The Dutch could easily have been three or four up by half time – but a kick off the line by Franchi and a full-length diving save by Pincher kept England's hopes alive – just.

'We're not keeping enough possession,' said Jimmy Stinger at half time. 'If we pass the ball like that for the rest of the game, we'll be swamped.'

'It's true you won't score goals if you're

trapped in and around your own penalty area,' said Jacky Dooley. 'But there were some good things out there – and we've got to build on them. For a start I want to see Headley and Cameron pushing up more. We're getting too compressed in front of the full backs and that makes it easy for them with their pace. I want more movement up the left to match the threat we're creating on the right side, understood?'

'But what about Van Hoof and Veenstra . . .' began Thomas.

'I know. They're dangerous, but if we attack more they'll be pushed back too. Hell, we're two goals down. There's no point in being negative.'

Thomas looked a little hurt until Jacky continued, 'Listen, son, you're as good as if not better than any Van Hoof or Veenstra. But your strength lies in going forward. Fair enough, you've got to defend like everyone else – but the front runners need you to link up with them.'

'OK,' said Thomas.

'Use a bit of muscle on them, Tommy,' said Jimmy Stinger as they walked out together for the re-start. 'Nothing too rough, mind – but get in hard. We need to play the English game; knock them out of their stride. And watch those passes. Don't give the ball away.'

Thomas knew that the England team and fans needed a goal to lift them at the beginning of the second half and he chased everywhere to nick possession from the Dutch. At last it paid off and he found Graham Deek with a curling pass down the left. Deekie held up the ball until Rory Cameron ran on to him, worked a one-two with Deek again and rolled the return pass beyond the Dutch defender who came on at him and, with all studs showing, up-ended the England player. Out came the yellow card and the ref pointed to a spot just outside the penalty area and left of centre – perfect for Ashleigh Coltrane.

Ashleigh lined up his shot, waited for the wall to move back, and then, as Dade stepped back into the row of Dutch defenders and ducked, he unleashed a curling shot directly through the gap. It swung viciously away from Gassmann's right hand into the left corner of the goal. Perfection, thought Thomas as he threw both arms around Ashleigh.

Holland immediately attacked again from the re-start and forced a corner on the left. It was taken short and Gresser found Van der Maas on the near post. His glancing header was going in when Pincher dived backwards and tipped over with the save of the tournament. The Holland players couldn't believe their eyes.

'Pincher is as good as our Rolly, I think,' said Van Hoof to Thomas as they trotted back together.

'Best goalie in the world,' said Thomas.

But he was soon to see Rolly Gassmann in

action at close quarters. Graham Deek broke down the wing and chipped back to Thomas whose first-time cross met the head of Coltrane as he dived forward. 'Goal,' screamed Thomas and the crowd together and then there was an even louder groan as Gassmann managed to parry the ball with one fist. It was a reaction-save out of the top drawer and he followed it with a tip over as Dade struck a wonderful drive from the clearance.

The disappointment didn't dampen the growing optimism of the England fans and they roared on the white shirts. The tempo rose and the controlled passing game of the Dutch began to break up slightly. Suddenly they were giving England more possession and the midfield battle became even more intense. Rory Cameron was having the game of his life. Time and again his searching passes put Holland on the back foot and Coltrane, Deek and Dade were, at last, getting the service they needed. But still the Dutch were dangerous on the break and Pincher was called into action again to pull off a huge save when Kraal again broke clear. Two–one it stayed, however.

The Wembley turf was taking its toll on the players and more and more mistakes were creeping in. Jacky Dooley brought Rutherford Stacey on for Francie Ramsay to provide some fresh legs at the back and immediately Bazza Taylor went down injured after yet another saving tackle. He tried to run it off but it was his hamstring, and when Kraal beat him for pace through the middle, Jacky realised he had to take him off.

But now the England manager was in serious trouble. He was left with only one midfielder and two forwards on the bench and the midfield player, Ray Clooney, hadn't kicked a ball in the tournament. Joss Morecombe suggested the solution.

The 3–5–2 formation put a lot of pressure on Thomas and Jimmy Stinger to run the wings but it was the only answer. With the game stretched out from end to end Thomas found himself covering more ground than he'd ever seen on a football

field before. Thank God I'm fit, he thought, as he stormed up the left once again after tackling back to his own goal line. He looked up at the big scoreboard. Five minutes to play. Cameron found him with a perfect ball down the touchline. He kept it in play and stormed up field with Van Hoof shadowing him on the inside. Thomas shaped to cut back and ran on. The dummy gave him half a yard on his marker and he sensed Dade and Coltrane running into space in the centre. The cross felt good, it had weight and curve. Thomas fell as he dispatched the ball and Van Hoof landed on top of him. He just glimpsed Dade coming in on the ball and meeting it with his head. Then he heard the crowd roar and he knew the scores were level.

Van Hoof spat out something in Dutch and then helped Thomas sportingly to his feet. 'Long time since I've been left like that,' he said. 'You're quick.'

'Extra time?' said Thomas.

'Maybe,' said the Dutchman. 'But still we win.'

But the 90 minutes had not yet given up its full portion of drama. From the centre kick England gained possession down the right and Stinger sent in a speculative cross from the right. Deek got to the ball first and fired in a shot from just inside the area which was blocked. The rebound flew to Thomas who was racing in from the left. WHAM! He hit it on the volley. The shot, struck at hip height, could have gone anywhere. But, almost in disbelief, Thomas watched it travel like a bullet towards the far post. It struck the post, rebounded off the diving keeper and shot into the back of the net. Three–two.

The crowd howled its delight. The game came to a halt whilst the entire England team congratulated Thomas and Jimmy Stinger tried to get them concentrating again. 'Three minutes and probably a couple of minutes of extra time,' he kept saying over and over.

The Dutch weren't finished. They ran at the tiring English defence, but the thin white line held and held ... and then Van der Maas fired in another speculative shot and Franchi headed off the line only to see Rudi Kraas nip in and fire a volley from 10 yards which even Sean couldn't get a hand to. The scenes of dejection and delirium on and off the pitch were amazing. Within seconds the ref had blown for the end of normal time. Three–three was the score that flashed out on the big new Wembley scoreboard.

So extra time it was and maybe penalties after that. The players slumped gratefully to the ground at the final whistle and waited for the trainers and the physios to come on. They watched as the big screen re-ran the last three goals. Thomas enjoyed his first proper view of Freddy's brilliant header and was even more transfixed at the sight of his own cracking volley. If only the game had ended then and there . . .

Some of the players were suffering from cramp. Jason had lost a tooth in a collision, Dave Franchi had a black eye from an elbowing and Jimmy Stinger was limping slightly but had no intention of going off. 'I could run around this pitch for a year if it meant coming back with the Cup,' he said to Jacky.

'Then keep running, skipper, ' said Jacky. The manager issued no further instructions. 'You're doing great, keep pressuring them,' he said. It was clear that Jacky favoured snatching the golden goal rather than going through the penalty ordeal.

The re-start came all too soon and the players dragged themselves back to their positions still breathing hard from the effort of the game. England were nearly caught on the hop by a quick break but Sean came to their rescue. The Dutch had regained their composure and they were closing down the England players at every opportunity. Another attack by Holland produced a stunning Pitcher save. From the corner Veenstra nearly scrambled the ball over the goal line and it took a quick piece of work by Franchi to get it clear. The teams changed around with the score still 3–3.

Jacky contemplated a substitution but decided against it. Holland brought on two subs and immediately their extra pace up front caused problems for the tiring back row. Sean again saved his side from defeat by chasing out and diving at the feet of Kraal, who was free, on the edge of the area. The minutes were ticking away and a penalty shoot-out loomed – it was clearly on the minds of all the players.

Franchi cleared again and this time he found Graham Deek on the halfway line. Thomas chased forward again. Last time, he thought. As he burst into the Holland half Deek pushed a long, searching ball ahead of him. Just onside, thought Thomas. There was no whistle. The race was on. Would Thomas have the legs to get to the ball ahead of the Dutch centre back? He stuck out a leg and touched it past the defender and jumped over the tackle. Two players converged on him. A sidestep and a swerve, then a dummy the other way, took him clean past them. Rolly Gassmann was off his line, narrowing the angle, but Thomas knew it was now or never. The ball was on his left foot and he cracked it with the outside of his boot. It swerved viciously away from the keeper and then further. For an instant it seemed it would swing beyond the post. But no. The ball evaded Gassmann's fingers by inches and brushed the inside of the left-hand post. GOAL!

If there had ever been a bigger roar at Wembley it would have lifted off the roof and left the entire

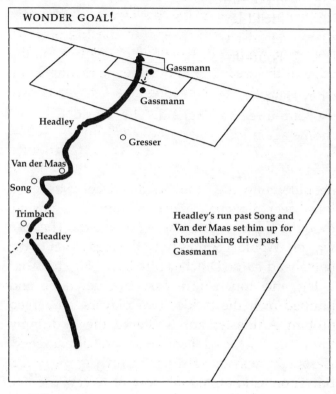

WONDER GOAL!

Gassmann

Gassmann

Headley

Gresser

Van der Maas

Song

Trimbach

Headley

Headley's run past Song and Van der Maas set him up for a breathtaking drive past Gassmann

○ Holland
● England

crowd deafened for life. Thomas chased after the ball into the net and the whole England team followed in after him. As they rolled around and became entangled in the netting, the crowd went crazy.

'Four–three
Head-ley
Head-ley
Four–three'

they sang.

Four–three to England. The World Cup was home again.

11
THE MORNING AFTER

It was all a dream. It had to be.

In the space of scarcely three months Thomas Headley had run around the great national arena holding first the FA Cup and now the World Cup. At the age of only 18 he was a sporting legend throughout the world. What more could he achieve? To have touched the twin pinnacles of his career so early would surely blight him for the rest of his footballing life. Many would reflect on that in days to come. But not today – today was for celebrations and for glory. The nation saluted their heroes. Less than two hours of football, it seemed, had changed the world and the 19 young men who had made that happen could ask for anything they liked today. In the eyes of a grateful, joyous nation they could do no wrong. Everyone wanted to see them, to be with them, to share in their astonishing triumph.

As Thomas awoke he lazily recalled the high points of the Wembley victory: the battling second half; the calm captaincy of Jimmy Stinger; the command of the back four and Sean Pincher's heroics in goal; Rory Cameron's growing authority in midfield and the endless running and battling of Coltrane, Dade and Deek. But most of all he remembered his two goals. Would he ever forget them? Particularly the second one, the ball hit on the run – he could still feel it on his left foot, the timing perfect, only a few inches of space to aim at and by some miracle he got it spot on. He replayed it in his mind's eye time and time again.

Then there was the ceremony: going up to receive the Jules Rimet trophy from the Queen and the victory salute around Wembley with the crowd roaring them on, with perhaps the biggest roar of all when Thomas took the Cup and held it out to the England supporters behind the posts where he'd scored the golden goal.

But most of all Thomas remembered the words of Jacky Dooley as he and Joss Morecombe and the entire squad stood in front of the television cameras. He could have been triumphant and gloating. Many in the media had done nothing to support him in his hour of need; on the contrary, they had hounded him and made his job ten times harder. But there was no crowing, no trace of boastfulness. Instead Jacky spoke in his usual quiet, calm voice, 'I can't begin to thank all the people who made this happen. There are some young lads in this team who have behaved like wise old warriors and some older players who have run their legs off like young terriers. And they've had the most fantastic support from the fans, from you people in the press and from the trainers, physios and administration team. Sometimes I think I've had the easiest job of all. And right now I think it's the best job in the world.

'Just one more thing. We played well but we got the breaks, too. It takes great teams to make a great tournament, and my heart goes out to the players and managers who weren't quite as lucky as us. Especially the brave Holland team and their manager, Klaus – I thought they were brilliant and if they'd been standing here right now as victors, no one could have said they weren't worthy of it.'

Today Jacky and Joss and the squad would be back together again; there would be more victory parades – the biggest one on an open top bus travelling through the streets of the capital. Afterwards there would be a huge gathering in Hyde Park, where no doubt the politicians would congratulate themselves on winning the World Cup for England. Thomas didn't care about that. He rolled over in bed. His body was tired; it had been the most exhausting and wearing month of football in his life. But tiredness didn't matter now; the pain was worth it. Winning was the thing and he promised himself that he would never forget how good it felt to win at the very highest level.

England's World Cup Record:

Group Games

England 4	Nigeria 4
Headley, Coltrane,	*Ahime, Ekinki (2),*
Deek, Stinger	*Olawande*

England 1	United States 1
Stilton	*Weinberg*

England 3	France 2
Dade, Deek,	*Rammasseur (2)*
Headley	

Quarter-final

Argentina 0	England 1
	Le Braz

Semi-final

England 2	Italy 2
Deek (2)	*Mirandola, Malpiero*

(England won 4–3 on penalties)

Final

England 4   Holland 3
(after extra time)
Coltrane, Dade,   *Kraal (3)*
Headley (2)

Top Goal Scorers

Kraal (Holland)	7
Malpiero (Italy)	5
Rammasseur (France)	5
Dade (England)	4
Deek (England)	4
Headley (England)	4
Ekinki (Nigeria)	4
Tomaso (Brazil)	4

Joint 'Players of the Tournament'
(selected by the international press)

Thomas Headley (England)
Rudi Kraal (Holland)